Journey Time

Paul G. Diamond

Disclaimer

For Nicki, Eleanor, James and Ronnie

"In serious fiction, where the writer feels he's accomplishing something besides simply amusing people - although there's nothing wrong with simply amusing people - the writer is holding up a mirror to the human species, making it possible for you to understand people better because you've read the novel or story, and maybe making it possible for you to understand yourself better. That's an important thing.

Now science fiction uses a different method. It works up an artificial society, one which doesn't exist, or one that may possibly exist in the future, but not necessarily. And it portrays events against the background of this society in the hope that you will be able to see yourself in relation to the present society... That's why I write science fiction - because it's a way of writing fiction in a style that enables me to make points I can't make otherwise."

Isaac Asimov

Contents

Prologue

7.11pm
Wednesday 5 December 2103

WALKING AND THINKING, I can't seem to do one without the other.

Right now I'm walking to the Community Hall to prepare for tonight's group and, for no apparent reason, I'm thinking about all the people I don't know.

"The list of people I don't know is endless," I think to myself.

The same is true for everyone of course, especially when you think about the billions of people around the world. You don't know them and they don't know you. But I was thinking locally. I've lived round here for nearly seven years and every time I leave the house, the first person I see is always someone new.

"What does that say about me?"

I ask myself questions like this all the time.

"It probably says, Steve, you need to get out more."

I know I need to up my social game.

I've tried forcing myself to stop thinking but it just leads to more thoughts.

"You're too easily distracted," is the latest to flash through my mind.

I ignore it and focus on walking instead.

I look around me. The road I'm walking along is quiet. There are tall trees to one side, I think one is an Ash. I look down at the flag-stones, they are light-grey and even. I decide this is a good stretch of pavement, although maybe it's too narrow to comfortably pass someone coming the other way.

"This is what happens when I focus on walking," I think to myself again.

It's frustrating, and it can't be a good thing. Walking around with a full-blown conversation going on in my mind, oblivious to the world around me.

"Talking to myself isn't going to win me any new friends."

With this thought my mind is just mocking me.

From the outside I think I look normal enough while I'm walking. I might seem a little distracted and lost in my thoughts. Perhaps I do look withdrawn.

"You look like you could use a good meal," my Grandma used to say.

I guess not having much meat on my bones comes from living alone and cooking for one. And from missing out on all those restau-rant meals I used to enjoy.

Now my mind runs away with the subject of restaurant meals.

I always found the company much more interesting than the food.

"Give me great friends in an average restaurant every day," I think to myself.

"Unless the food is awful, although awful food makes great conversation."

Nice going Steve, another throwaway thought.

The trouble is I'll hoard it instead of throwing it away. I'm like a magpie with a nest full of shiny things, although I collect thoughts and questions in my head.

Treasuring them despite their lack of any practical use.

"So this is how my mind works," I think, reaching for any kind of conclusion.

Outside of work, my life mainly consists of sitting around distracting myself. Then I dislocate myself even more as I walk from place to place. I try not to get distracted but anything and everything seems to spark a new flame. A bushfire of streaming consciousness is what usually follows, although that makes it sound far too exciting.

I try again to rein in my thoughts.

"Have you ever considered being thankful for the gift of a mind like yours?"

One of my mentors said this to me in a group session a few years ago. I should thank him again because it definitely helped. I'd always thought about my mind in a negative way before I heard this. Now I tend to focus on the upside of being a compulsive over-thinker. Nowadays, a lot more of my overactive thinking gets put to good use. Tonight's new group for example, I don't think I could support anyone if I didn't have the ability to obsess on their behalf.

"That's more like it," I think to myself.

Another advantage of having a restless mind comes to me.

"I'm good with complicated things."

An impulsive thought reminds me I'm useless at maths. Maybe 'complicated' was the wrong choice of word. My mind searches for a better example. It comes up with a game I used to play where an alien lands on earth and asks me to explain this strange new world.

For a while this game was my perfect waste of time.

"An introverted insomniac's dream," I say to myself, this time out loud.

I'm almost at the hall now but the alien explanation game has stayed on my mind. I remember why I stopped playing it, because I always hit a dead-end at ZJT.

Once again I find myself searching for an easier way to tell this part of the story.

"If you don't understand ZJT our world just doesn't make sense," how true I think to myself.

My mind sets about this familiar task once again. I imagine a new conversation word for word.

"Hello Mr. Alien. Sorry, Ms. Alien, I've never seen your species before so it's hard to tell. My name's Steve, I'm a human being. We run things around here and we're a pretty smart bunch. We used to live in caves, then we invented instantaneous matter transfer. It revolutionised our world but then it started making people sick so we switched it off and went back to the Stone Age. Maybe you can tell us where we went wrong? We'd be ever so grateful if you could."

"Complete and utter rubbish," I shake my head and tut as I arrive at the hall.

This was exactly why I stopped playing the alien game. Only I would put pressure on myself for the sake of a worthless fantasy.

Not being able to make sense of our world frustrates me all over again.

"I don't have all the answers but then again who does?"

Thinking this makes me feel slightly better.

I remind myself to stop struggling with questions the way an alcoholic reminds himself not to drink.

"Just try struggling less while you're out walking," my friend Kevin once said, "It makes you look odd."

This makes me laugh again as I walk into the hall. I'm first to arrive and begin setting up.

1

"Some people adjust easy.
Others prefer denial.
The rest of us choose Journey Time."
Elon Mensch

7.32pm
Wednesday 5 December 2103
Session 1

THE FLY ON the wall counted seven of us in the room. At least that's what I imagined she was doing.

Everyone is now here so it's time to get this brand new <u>Journey Time</u> programme underway. It's a small group by our standards, certainly small enough to make the Community Hall seem much larger than it is.

Before anyone arrived I set the chairs out in a small circle.

"Don't set them too close," Elena said in my leadership training. "<u>The handbook</u> specifies half-metre spacing on either side."

Elena was a great coach. There's no way I'd be here tonight without her support. It still makes me feel better when I imagine her voice in my ear.

I'm the only one counting but this is my eleventh session as a JT group leader, only my second full programme in the chair. Whatever way I think about it, these numbers make me feel small.

For the last few minutes Kevin and I welcomed the new participants as they arrived. I'm always happy when Kevin's around to meet and greet with me. The two of us make a good team. He smiles broadly and shakes hands warmly. I smile awkwardly and make the tea.

It doesn't take long to make people feel welcome and get them settled in their chairs. Now this has been done we can begin.

I put down my cup and lean forward to speak.

"Welcome everyone to Journey Time session number one. I'm Steve and I'll be your group leader for the ten meetings we'll have together over the next five months."

I pause for a second to let the timescale sink in. Ten meetings and five months isn't much time but I know from experience how well the format works.

"The plan is to meet here, 7.30pm on Wednesdays, every other week. Everything else tends to fall into place if we get that part right."

I think to myself how unconvincing my voice sounds. I try to shake off this negative thought and get on with more of the standard introduction.

"The handbook will keep me on track," I think to myself.

The familiarity of the handbook's phrases immediately makes me feel better. Everyone who signs up for a JT programme gets the basic intro in an online induction but it feels good to go over some of this again, particularly to talk about grounding.

I talk about how grounding starts and what each member of the group will contribute.

The more I talk, the more relaxed I feel.

"The structure of our sessions is simple. Everything revolves around talking. When you're ready, you'll all take turns sharing experiences with the rest of the group. You tell your story in your own words."

I like to think this is what everyone was expecting. With that in mind I try sharing something new.

"One or two of you might leave before the ten sessions are up. Most of you will stay the course and get something out of it. It's not always what you expect but maybe that's the point. If we knew everything at the start none of us would be here."

I instantly wish I could take those last two sentences back. I just planted the idea of leaving into everyone's head. Worse than that, I introduced new doubts about what the programme achieves.

"Nice going Steve," I think to myself.

I try to get back on firmer ground as fast as I can.

"Because we're all new to each other, tonight's mainly a get-to-know-you session. To kick things off I'll introduce myself properly by sharing a personal story, then I'll introduce Kevin."

Kevin nodded and raised his hand in acknowledgement.

"As you already know, Kevin and I are your leadership team."

"Isn't two the smallest possible number for a team?" Kevin said, injecting a welcome note of relief.

I paused for some polite laughter before going on.

"Kevin will introduce himself properly, then we'll hear your intros around the room."

The youngest looking male squirmed in his cheap, plastic seat.

I reminded myself we needed to get some more comfortable chairs.

"Don't worry if you don't know what to say when it comes to your turn. If you get stuck, just say your name, how long it's been since your last zip and we'll move on from there," I said, making another deliberate effort to relax.

Breathing out slowly I reminded myself the worst was over. The session was up and running. No one had walked out. There was plenty of active listening and only one person had continually checked his quad-gpd.

"Not a bad start after all," I think to myself.

I finish my intro with a few words about the Journey Time ethos. I explain how the organisation was originally set up to help people build lives without a dependence on zip-travel. How the idea of being grounded came before the <u>big shutdown</u>, although it became a lot more prominent afterwards. I re-affirm the fact that neither Kevin nor I are psychotherapists. How we don't use any meds, neuro-linguistic programming, <u>AI implants</u> or any other tricks at any time throughout the course.

"All we will do is meet up, sit together and talk," I say to the group.

I continually look around the circle as I speak, trying to make eye contact wherever possible. At this early stage it is critical no one feels left out.

Even though this is only my second programme as a leader, I recognise the group's mannerisms well. All eyes take turns looking down, then darting from person to person. Arms are folded, hands are tucked away, feet are crossed and uncrossed, coffee cups tremble as they are lifted to lips. All of these are non-verbal signs of discomfort. Perfectly normal behaviour for first-time participants, and easy enough to spot when you know what to look for.

Kevin was the odd one out. His body language was warm, open and positive from the moment the first person stepped into the room. Right now he was sitting in the confident pose of a Journey Time Veteran. Relaxed and assured.

The handbook calls for one 'Vet' in every group. This rule is an absolute deal-breaker and applies even for group leaders with years of experience. I'd been a Vet for about a year before leading my first programme. I like the Vet system a lot. It works well and offers everyone huge levels of comfort.

It was time for Kevin and I to share our personal intro stories. According to the handbook, in no more than three and a half minutes we had to, "...give an authentic flavour of our personal journeys and explain how we ended up here today."

I'd shared stories so many times but each time it still felt different, even if I'd told the same story before. This kind of experience-sharing isn't like a speech you can rehearse and then repeat time and time again, it has a life of its own. I don't know why but when it's done right, something new always turns up in the telling.

During my training Elena had praised my personal stories. She said they sounded, "genuine and conversational". Then again Elena also said, "Stephen can sound like a parish priest trying to make his Sunday sermons more interesting." This comparison annoyed me at the time, until I got over myself and realised she was right.

Reliving this experience makes me smile. I take a sip of water and begin to speak.

"I suppose the best place to start is by saying I zipped for most of my life and I loved it. At least I loved it until about five years ago when I had my first paranoid freak-out. Not long after I was diagnosed with ZJT-d."

I remember how ashamed I used to feel about this illness. Now it's just part of my story.

"After being diagnosed I cut down my travel but also I started what I now call my 'search for meaning'."

I made the bunny-ears quote sign with my fingers as I said this. Kevin stifled a laugh as I continued.

"It wasn't a planned thing at first, I just zipped to spiritual places. Hindu temples, Buddhist shrines, stone circles, ley-lines, cathedrals, if it was holy I went there. I also zipped to sunrises all over the world. There was nothing like zjt for that. '100 Dawns a Day' as Step'N'Go used to say."

This fond memory of an old ad campaign helps to calm my nerves.

"I zipped to sunsets, desert islands, wildernesses, mountaintops, the middle of jungles, the centre of almost every big city. Then one day I checked my stats and they registered 339,085 total zips. A 33.2 life-time daily average. Not the highest numbers by any means but after all those places I'd been, I still hadn't found what I was looking for."

I paused to let this realisation sink in once again. At the time, seeing these numbers on my quad made me feel lost. They physically shook me and I didn't know why. I hoped my storytelling was doing this justice. It's taken me a long time to get here but nowadays there's nothing I want to hide.

"It's hard to explain but those numbers were my wake up call. After seeing them my life didn't make sense any more. I lost the desire to go anywhere. Nothing interested me the same way. I couldn't connect with people or places, even if I loved them before. Looking back, it's the closest I ever came to <u>full-d</u>."

I made a quick check around the room. Everyone was paying attention. Kevin gave me a wink, encouraging me to go on.

"A few weeks later I went to my first JT session. About six months after my grounding the first big <u>RC</u> scare broke. Not long after that the whole <u>grid</u> came down," I said.

The shutdown was a significant, shared life event for us all. Everyone remembered where they were when it happened. Everyone had a personal shutdown story. I always include the shutdown in my intros. New participants need to know they have plenty in common with each other and their group leaders.

I started bringing my story to a close.

"As for where I am today, I've got a lot better at living in one place. I go on long walks and have got to know the local area better. Walking has also given me a new perspective on journey time. It this might not sound like much but this all feels like progress to me."

I think about how this is true. How I feel better in so many ways.

"New destinations no longer define who I am. You might laugh, but now I even know some of my neighbours."

I tried to make this a joke by lifting my voice at the end of the sentence but no one laughed.

I make a mental note to leave the jokes to Kevin before carrying on.

"Today this neighbourhood is part of my life. Journey Time helped me appreciate this. My zip-travel life wasn't all bad but it wasn't my life. Zip-travel owned me. I used to be everywhere, but in reality I was nowhere."

The group seemed to understand this feeling. I clung to it as another positive sign.

"Getting grounded with JT has brought me this far. I still have some work to do but I've come a long way and I'm looking forward to the journey ahead," I said, bringing my intro to a close.

I gave myself an immediate review. My story ended positively but it was by no means my greatest performance. The middle part sounded heavy on the spiritual, which isn't the JT way. Mysticism is definitely not in the handbook.

I didn't want my efforts being judged in silence for too long so I handed over to Kevin straight away. Kevin is more of a natural at this stage than me.

"Who am I trying to kid, Kevin's more of a natural all-round," I think to myself.

I remember refusing to lead any group with Kevin in it. I was too intimidated, until he put me at ease. Kevin had spoken straight to my fears before our first leadership programme together.

"I want you to lead and me to Vet," he said, "And I won't have it any other way."

It didn't matter how much I argued with him. Nor how many times I told him about the mess I would make, Kevin wouldn't change his mind.

Returning from my thoughts, I sat back to listen and watch the group as Kevin spoke.

"I remember my first session like it was yesterday. There's usually one reluctant participant in each programme, and in my first group it was me."

Kevin looked around the circle as he spoke.

"I'd never been to any 'talk-it-out' meetings before. It was Saira's idea for me to go. She knew about JT and thought it would help 'my addiction' as she called it. The fact I couldn't stay in one place for any length of time."

Everyone watched Kevin. Even the 'fiddling-with-his-quad' guy was now paying attention.

"Like Steve, I came to JT before the shutdown. As my programme went on, I started to feel like I was in the right place after all. Not just in the sessions but at home as well. I was spending more of my time locally and it wasn't driving me mad."

Kevin paused for a moment, something he did before stressing a point.

"After the shutdown the option to zip-out wasn't there anymore but by then I was already zipping less. I guess what I'm saying is being in one place, with a little <u>hard-travel</u> here and there, grew on me."

As if he was talking to friends he'd known for years, Kevin finished his intro with an amiable shrug. Everyone had listened closely to Kevin, although I did notice one of the smartly dressed females was now looking anxious. She'd been moving around in her seat while Kevin was speaking. Now she was also messing with her quad.

With Kevin's intro done, I looked around the room and asked if anyone wanted to go first with theirs. No one volunteered so I suggested we go clockwise around the circle, starting with the person to my right. One by one everyone took turns to say 'Hello' and say their name. Around the circle we heard Agnieszka, Oran, Mila, Royar and Arle all speak for the first time.

A few seconds after introducing herself, Arle's quad sounded with a loud message tone.

All eyes switched to her as she checked the screen.

"I'm sorry," Arle said, grabbing her bag as she stood up, "I have to go."

Arle was already on her way to the door before I could say anything. Kevin motioned for me to keep going and followed her out of the hall.

I carried on with the session but found it hard not to think about Arle. A participant walking out was never good news. I hoped she hadn't left because of something I said. My paranoia turned up the heat as I imagined Arle could easily be a mystery-participant from JT head office. She had seemed rushed more than anything else as she left.

None of these thoughts were helping me talk to the group. My immediate response was to say that a participant choosing to leave was nothing out of the ordinary.

"It proves we're only here because we want to be. All of us are free to leave at any time," I said, then I realised this sounded like an invitation, so I added the statistic that 63% of leavers re-join the same group later in the programme, or sign up again at a later date.

Agnieszka asked a couple of questions in response to this. On the whole people seemed satisfied with the explanation. As we were talking Kevin came back through the door. With a shake of his head in my direction I knew Arle wasn't coming back.

"It happens," Kevin said to the group as a whole, "Arle will have her reasons."

Royar laughed quietly at this but kept the joke to himself.

We needed to talk about Arle but I didn't want 'leaving' to be our focus for too long. I decided it was a good time to call an early break, although I added an icebreaker task to get everyone back to thinking as a unit. The task I set was for each participant to remember a childhood story, preferably one where some kind of life-lesson was learned. The plan was to share these stories when we returned.

This icebreaker was of course straight out of the handbook. It was a great way to introduce new participants to personal sharing. It was also my favourite elective, early-stage element and I usually found a good reason to squeeze it in. Tonight that reason was Arle.

• • •

I wasn't at all surprised with the way the group broke up for coffee. Royar walked to one corner of the room to make a call. Mila and Oran went outside for some fresh air. Agnieszka stayed in the circle making notes, I assumed they were notes for her story.

When we got back together Agnieszka volunteered to share first. She spoke with a clear voice as she read from her quad.

"In my second year of school I won an award for being the most helpful student. I won because I used to visit an elderly neighbour every morning. I also used to help new kids settle in to their classes. It was nice to win the award but the reason I was so helpful as a kid was because of my Mum," Agnieszka looked up from her screen, thinking as she spoke.

"My Mum used to say, 'Help others with a good heart Annie, and one day you'll realise they were helping you.' I'm not sure I completely understood what she meant but I knew she was right."

The group seemed to enjoy Agnieszka's story. In hindsight she was the ideal person to go first because she pitched her story just right. Not too long, not too short, just the right amount of intimacy for session number one.

I always breathe a little sigh of relief when a first-time participant shares. Every contribution adds to the personality of the group, while lifting some of the pressure from Kevin and myself. If I could have an Agnieszka in every programme I'd be over the moon.

Encouraged by these new feelings of progress I asked Royar if he wanted to go next. Royar agreed. Like Agnieszka he was also a comfortable speaker, perhaps he was even more assured. I hadn't warmed to Royar's manners up to now but as he began speaking I couldn't help liking his voice.

"My Dad and I cycled across the US when I was 11," Royar said with the faintest hint of a smile.

"He said he wanted me to experience enough journey to last a lifetime. He wanted to teach me that travel was a complete waste of time."

An affectionate look crossed Royar's faced before vanishing as quickly as it came.

"To my Dad there were only ever two points on a journey. Departure and arrival. He used to say, 'nothing but wasted time exists in between'."

Royar looked at me to signal his story had finished.

Although there was no doubting his confidence, Royar looked relieved to be done.

Two stories in, the second half of this session felt much better than the first. We took some time to explore Agnieszka and Royar's experiences around the circle. Royar didn't have much more to say but Agnieszka was happy to answer a few of my questions.

Oran and Mila asked if they could have more time to think about their childhood stories. I was happy to move this task onto our agenda for the next session. Agnieszka asked if Kevin and I were going to share a childhood story. This was always part of our plan but I was glad it wasn't implicit. It worked far better to say yes to Agnieszka and submit to the will of the group, which we did. Kevin and I both agreed to share in the next session, although with a little time to go, Kevin offered to share his childhood story tonight.

The story Kevin told was new to me too.

"When I was seven, I threw a pear at a wasps' nest. It didn't take me long to figure out this was a dumb thing to do."

Kevin spoke slowly, making no attempt to gloss over his own foolishness.

"Later that day the exterminators came to get rid of the nest. When he put me to bed my Dad had a sad look on his face. He told me they'd found a bird's nest with three dead chicks in it. All of the chicks had been stung to death by the wasps."

There was noticeable discomfort in Kevin's voice.

"I cried when he told me. The guilt of killing a family of birds hurt me so much more than the stings. My Dad said he wasn't going to tell me about the nest because I'd already learned my lesson. But in the end he did because it would teach me about the law of unintended consequences, particularly when you do stupid things."

The group stayed quiet after Kevin stopped speaking. I thought about Kevin as a child. It was hard to imagine he was ever a destructive kid. As I was thinking the conversation started up again.

Agnieszka spoke to Kevin about her Mother and his Father.

"I think they would have got on," she said laughing.

Forgetting his need for more time Oran dived into a story of his own, although Mila and I were the only ones listening. Royar might have been listening too but he was keeping one eye on his quad. I wondered what he was looking at and why it was so important. I wanted to tell him to put the device away but that wasn't JT policy.

As it says in the handbook, "Let people quad all they like, there's no better sign of dislocation."

Back in the room, the livelier exchanges continued all the way to our finishing time and a few minutes beyond. At this stage of the programme there's nothing more pleasing than a little bit of flow.

When the time came to bring the session to a close, I handed a blank journal to every participant. These pocket-sized notebooks are the low-tech equivalent of the JT apps and resources the group had installed on their quads. I encouraged each participant to use either their soft or hard journal and to start using it between now and our next session.

"What you write doesn't matter. That you write does," I read the quote from Elon Mensch out loud, pointing to it on the inside cover of each journal. I also explained why journaling is such an important part of the programme and a big part of every individual grounding process.

Oran took a silver pen from his pocket and started writing in his journal immediately.

· · ·

After the last group member left the hall, Kevin and I cleared up.

I added the chairs to the stacks at the end of the room while he washed the cups. With our chores done we made our way out and I locked up the hall. I couldn't wait to ask Kevin about Arle and now the carrying, clinking and jangling was over, this was my first question on our walk home.

"She definitely didn't want to talk," Kevin said in reply. "She'd folded up her quad and was pretty much running down the path."

We crossed the road without looking up. There was never any traffic here anyway.

"I chased after her to see if she was OK. Without stopping she pointed to her quad, told me it was an important call and she had to go. That's all." Kevin shrugged his shoulders.

"That's all?" I said, hoping there would be more.

"There was something else," Kevin interrupted my growing sense of frustration. I think he enjoyed making me wait.

"Arle said her father was right, JT is full of freaks. I guess fifteen minutes with us was all she needed to decide this was true."

Kevin and I both laughed, it wasn't the first time we'd heard this point of view.

"And it was all going so well," I said, half-joking, half-seeking reassurance from Kevin.

"It was a good start and a much better finish. Don't worry about Arle. When someone decides to walk, no one can stop them. You know we're not even supposed to try."

Kevin's logic was comforting to hear.

We walked on and talked about the rest of the group. The top of my road was the usual point where we went our separate ways. When we arrived, Kevin had his parting shot ready. He liked to have the last word on our walks home, and he liked it to lighten the mood.

"You know Steve, I think Arle may have blipped her quad on purpose after your intro," Kevin said, with a playful grin on his face.

"It's that whole Buddhist temple, search-for-meaning thing. Not everyone gets it."

Kevin was already walking away.

"Maybe I should put that on the 'don't-tell' list," I said to Kevin's back as he walked up the hill.

"Might be an idea. See you in a few weeks," he said, raising his arm without turning around.

I walk the last few minutes home trying to think of better intro stories. Then it crosses my mind Kevin was winding me up. This thought makes me laugh, mainly because it always shows up five minutes too late.

2

"Join JT to help yourself.
Stay to help others."
Elon Mensch

**7.25pm
Wednesday 19 December 2103
Session 2**

TWO WEEKS HAVE gone by in no time at all. I haven't done much walking since the last session. I haven't done much of anything except throw myself into the lives and personalities of this new group. Without doubt this is one of my favourite parts of the job.

"Sanctioned preoccupation," Elena used to call it. Of course she was right.

Even though I'd only met the new participants once, I had no problem spending hours thinking about them. I find it impossible not to speculate on the different qualities of each person every time I lead a new group. At this stage there are so many more questions than answers. So many possible outcomes, so many things to discover, so many ways to imagine each individual journey unfolding.

Tonight, as the minutes tick down to the start of the new session, I'm thinking about each participant again. I go over what I have learned so far, at the same time cautioning myself that the evidence of one meeting only goes so far.

"Don't lose sight of the line between evidence and facts," I remind myself.

I hold onto this the way a climber holds rope.

In the run up to my first leadership programme Kevin and I chatted a lot. Looking back I was pretty much a nervous wreck. My biggest fear was people walking out, or worse still that no one would share anything. As usual, Kevin made me feel a lot better.

Among the many things Kevin said to me was, "There's always someone who says nothing in session one."

I laughed when Kevin said this because in my first session this was me.

Mila had been our non-talker this time around, although I wasn't worried about her finding her voice. Of the other participants only Oran had any potential to be talkative. Royar, or Roy as he asked to be called, was quiet but confident when he did speak. I always found this an interesting combination. I'd seen it before but the reasons behind it were never the same.

Kevin had already nicknamed Royar 'Yar'. For some reason he found this really funny but I didn't get the joke. For most of the first session Royar just looked bored. He was definitely the group's reluctant Journey Timer so far. Apart from when he was listening to Kevin's story, Royar's feet shifted continually. Elena taught me to watch people's feet during sessions.

"If their feet are moving they want to get the hell out of there," Elena said. "There's no better way to read someone's mind."

Throughout our last session Royar couldn't keep his eyes off his quad. I thought about this again. Perhaps he was willing the grid to come back on. Maybe he regretted not walking out before Arle. Maybe he was checking his investments. Maybe he was just staring at his quad in the vain hope something might happen.

I had no idea what was on Royar's mind but it didn't stop me going over the possibilities.

Mila was the youngest member of the group. Unlike Royar she was interested in what others had to say. Mila also appeared to be taking everything in. She listened closely and made occasional notes throughout the first session. Kevin told me she was also swiping back and forth between her notepad and the CdA grid site during the break. I wasn't sure about the significance of this but I was glad Kevin told me. It might only be a small detail but it was another piece of the puzzle to play around with.

• • •

Everyone was now at the hall.

A little small talk had made sure the atmosphere wasn't awkward while Kevin and I made hot drinks and settled people in. I allowed myself one final reflection on how I'd used my time over the last two weeks.

"Would these people think it was creepy if they knew how much I'd been thinking about them? Would they see it as professional dedication? Would they expect any less?" I thought to myself.

I also thought how this job provided the perfect pastime for me. Most of my spare time could easily be eaten up this way. I left my thoughts where they were and began the session with a quick recap. I'd barely begun before Oran jumped in to update us on his journaling over the last fortnight.

Oran told us about a recent flight he took to Canada. It was the first time he had flown long-haul and he'd never been so bored in his life.

"If you want to learn about journey time, sit in coach-class for eight hours," was how he summed up the experience.

We discussed Oran's flight within the circle. Only Royar and Kevin had ever been on a plane so the conversation petered out before it ever really got started. Oran was more than happy to embellish his story with tales of his jet-lag. He made it sound like an exotic disease. Oran laid it on so thick Kevin asked if he'd been read his last rites. Everyone around the circle laughed at this.

Some people however were keen to move on.

"So when are we going to hear your remarkable childhood story Steve?" Royar said.

This was his dry way of telling us he was ready for a change of subject. Royar had no issue talking over Oran, although Oran took this as an invitation to stay in the spotlight and share his story first.

"I have so many stories but the lesson from this one really stands out," Oran said.

Oran's tone was verging on smug. So far he had enjoyed talking about himself more than anything else.

"I was talking to an Uncle at a family party, some old guy who didn't look too well" Oran said with a casual wave.

"I showed him one of my books about famous artists and he got emotional telling me about this house with an attic full of junk."

I noticed there was less and less compassion for Oran's Uncle in his tone.

"He was working for a removals firm to clear the house. It was winter and the movers lit a fire in the garden to keep warm. My Uncle told me they found some oil paintings in the loft but one of the guys he worked with threw them on the fire. My book reminded him of this and that's why he got upset."

My sympathy for Oran's Uncle continued growing as Oran carried on his story.

"I felt sorry for him, standing there watching those paintings burn. But I felt worse for the people who threw the paintings on the fire. Anyone who doesn't appreciate art must have such a miserable, empty life."

Oran didn't sound sorry for anyone in his story. Dismissive was closer to the truth. I wasn't sure what lesson Oran was sharing here. I thought maybe he was confused about the task or that his story might not be over. None of this mattered because Oran had already moved on to talk about his own love of art and how important this is now he works in the technology department for an international auctioneer.

Oran went on to explain how he had specialised in <u>ZJTTP</u> technology for this firm before the shutdown. Everyone found this much more interesting than his story. I watched Oran as he fielded questions from around the circle. He was delighted to be the centre of attention. I carried on thinking as this exchange went on.

Oran's childhood story had sounded truthful enough but it also sounded well worn, like he'd told it a number of times. I had no idea why a story like this would be repeated. I wondered if it was a story he used to tell people at work. On the whole, Oran didn't seem to care much for his audience. He made no noticeable attempt to follow what they were thinking or feeling. There were also unflattering notes of superiority in the way he spoke.

Not wanting to get carried away with my thoughts about Oran, I switched my attention back to the conversation. It struck me the entire session could be taken up by Oran reminiscing. One reason Kevin and I were here was to prevent something like this from happening. Although the group needed people who were happy to share, it also needed balancing so no one would feel left out.

I decided to step in by thanking Oran for his contributions, although this was just a gentle way to cut him off. Before Oran could take this as a slight, I followed up by asking Mila if she was ready to share her childhood story. It was a big relief when Mila said yes.

Mila had made handwritten notes in her physical journal. I thought to myself what a revelation these low-tech notebooks have been. It wasn't my thing but some people found pen and paper more personal than a quad. As she got ready to speak Mila rested the journal on her lap. Holding it in her hands was definitely comforting her.

Mila's fingers smoothed down the pages, keeping the paper flat as she started to read.

"My Mum loved zip-travel but she also had this habit of zipping back home several times a day. When I was young we did this back-and-forth all the time. I never really figured out why."

Mila continued reading word-for-word from her notes.

"Mum carried this on even after my brother and I left home. It didn't put me off zip-travel but I think about those unnecessary trips all the time."

Mila's voice softened, then faltered. It became an effort to hear her clearly.

"Mum died from RC three years ago. I can't help wondering if one of her zips back home was the cause."

Mila's head dropped. She pressed a tear from each eye with her forefinger and thumb. Agnieszka immediately went over to Mila, bobbing down at her side and placing an arm round her shoulders. I looked over to Kevin who knew exactly what to do. He went over to Alice and Mila while I suggested a quick comfort break. Oran and Royar immediately approved.

While Kevin and Agnieszka stayed with Mila I went over to the kitchen to fetch a glass of water and put the kettle on.

"The kettle, a uniquely British coping device," I thought to myself, although I knew this was a distraction from what was going on.

I wasn't aware at first but Royar had followed me over to the kitchen. I saw him when I turned around to take the water back to Mila. I acknowledged Royar on my return and got the feeling he was here to pick a bone with me. I silently hoped it wasn't to continue a conversation he been having with Kevin just before the session started.

At the weekend, over a hundred spectators were killed at a sports arena in Paris. The news was still sketchy on details but some anti-republique extremists were already claiming responsibility. Royar had spoken to Kevin in strong terms about hunting down the people responsible. Kevin had said it was always difficult to understand why these things happened. Both their voices had been loud enough for the rest of us to hear.

Royar was now leaning against the kitchen counter casually tapping the screen of his quad.

"So Steve, I guess you also think people who kill innocent members of the public need to be understood?"

Royar spoke without looking up from his screen. He assumed I'd been listening earlier. I didn't see any reason to hide what I overheard.

"If you're talking about what Kevin said earlier, I agree with him. We should try to learn more before a military response." I said in reply.

Although I would never have chosen this topic I did want Royar to engage. Maybe this could be the start of him playing a more active role in the group.

"Why Steve?" Royar's tone was serious. "Tell me what we can learn from murderers and terrorists."

Royar confirmed my suspicion he was over here to pick a fight. Being hunted down by Royar makes me think of the times when I was bullied as a child. Some of the physical and verbal attacks come back to mind. I remember the bruises the same way Kevin talked about his wasp stings. They never hurt as much as the guilt, or the shame.

"Maybe I was lucky to have bullies who didn't hit so hard," I thought to myself.

Despite trying to joke my way out of it, the shame comes flooding back, along with all the different methods of fighting back I tried, before finding the only one I could live with.

Now wasn't the best time but I gave in and stopped trying to fight off the emotion.

Back then I was scared. More than once I hit out. I even tried bullying other people to see if it was the answer. The memory of this hurts me all over again.

I think of Kevin's baby birds and the unintended harm I caused.

"People who use intimidation are always scared," I try to collect myself with this thought.

This is one of the most painful lessons I ever learned because I had to intimidate people in order to learn it. Remembering this makes me feel a new kind of shame. I force myself to think about how I recovered from all this as a child. How I rejected Royar's way as soon as I was able.

At last my redeeming thought arrives.

"I know Royar is scared."

Now I can stop myself replying to Royar in kind.

"There's always a reason for destructive behaviour," I say to Royar, doing my best to sound confident.

"We need to find out what's causing the violence," I add, stirring sugar into my coffee as I speak.

I wished Royar and I could talk about any subject other than this but it's a wish he isn't going to grant me.

"Come on Steve, is that what you really think?" Royar looks disappointed with me.

"You may as well put out the welcome mat for terrorists everywhere. Show that kind of weakness and everyone with a cause will pick up a rifle. Is that what you want?"

Royar was challenging me to defend my position. This was the kind of cut-and-thrust debate he enjoyed, although there was no enjoyment here for me.

"Of course I don't want that but we have to try and understand what's going on," I said.

I was absolutely convinced of this even if I didn't sound convincing. I had the feeling Royar would see this as new weakness to exploit. A comment like this would only make him bolder.

The thought of an emboldened Royar made me angry. I was angry with myself for allowing this to happen. I was behaving like a victim. As my frustration with myself rose, I wondered if Royar had ever used violence to dominate a situation. I thought about my immature attempts as a frightened child, to fight fire with fire, aggression with aggression. I think about splitting Royar's nose with the heel of my hand. I imagine the look of surprise on his face as he slides down the kitchen cabinet and slumps to the floor. Then I think about the chaos in the room and all the unwanted consequences this would cause. I would lose my job and be arrested for assault. My last thought was Royar suing me to penury, and how I would deserve it.

I knew my violent thoughts weren't voluntary. I remember reading about intrusive thoughts and how they can be perfectly normal.

Of course Royar wasn't in any danger. The last time I hit anyone I was thirteen years old.

Royar woke me from my thoughts by responding. He was definitely warming to his cause.

"I'm not sure you've really thought this through Steve. Look at these people who kill hundreds in the name of whatever it is they stand for. All they have to do is find a crowded place, a few explosives, automatic weapons and their pathetic cause is headline news. How many times does the same thing have to happen before people like you realise 'understanding' makes no difference?"

Royar mocked me by putting air quotes around the word 'understanding'. There was almost a sneer on his face as he steered our conversation towards a history of violence and terrorism that went back hundreds of years. I knew there would be no way out of this philosophical dead-end Royar was taking us down, but it didn't stop me trying.

"Perhaps you're right Roy. Maybe trying to understand elevates the terrorists and demeans us, but what else should we do? Killing just leads to more killing. Maybe killing even justifies their fight?"

I questioned whether I really believed this as Royar responded.

"The difference is we don't kill indiscriminately. You're forgetting we're in a fight for our lives."

Royar was absolutely convinced about this. This was the most involved I had seen him in any conversation, although he was still nowhere near losing his cool. I thought how it was his control I found most unsettling.

"I am in a fight Roy but not this fight. And I'm not fighting with you."

I knew Royar would hear this as an admission of defeat, which didn't bother me at all. I hoped Royar would now see me as feeble. He'd hardly even started the fight and I was rolling over. The look on his face was a picture of delight and mock sympathy. While Royar prepared what I imagined would be his victory speech, I asked myself why he needed this win over me. Why did he come over and restart this discussion? Was he doing it for the sake of his ego? Was it because he wasn't ready to submit to JT just yet? This all sounded possible but I must have made such a disappointing foe. Defeating me was hardly a triumph for someone like Royar. He would much rather cross swords with a worthy adversary like Kevin or Elon Mensch. Maybe it would be better for Royar if the JT CEO led this group. No doubt Royar could teach Mensch a thing or two.

While I was thinking, something in Royar's attitude changed. Maybe he decided I'd waved the white flag. Maybe he was satisfied his victory was already complete. Whatever the reason, with a great show of magnanimity Royar didn't press home his advantage. Instead he helped me carry the drinks over to the circle with a contented smile on his face.

I was quite sure everyone had caught the end of our exchange because it was quiet when Royar and I sat down. I was also sure this conversation with Royar was over but to my surprise it was Agnieszka who brought it back again.

"I used to work with a guy who loved playing devil's advocate," Agnieszka looked at Royar as she spoke.

"I thought it was fun for a while but I decided, if your heart's not in an argument, there's no point getting involved."

Agnieszka was directing her comments towards Royar. I watched as he calculated his response. She hadn't gone for him in an all-out attack so I guessed Royar would give Agnieszka the benefit of the doubt. Part of me wanted to see him flip and start yelling, although I knew this would never happen. Royar was too cagey to out himself as an aggressor.

In any event Agnieszka didn't give Royar more plotting time.

"About two-hundred years ago the British army killed hundreds of unarmed protestors in Amritsar. It wasn't a football match but the differences to Paris pretty much end there."

Agnieszka let this new information sink in before continuing.

"The British commanding officer claimed his actions were necessary to maintain order, which is another word for control. Killing hundreds of people was his way of staying in control. It's no different today."

Royar looked stunned by the comparison Agnieszka was making.

"The violence is the same. The outrage is the same. And it's all happening for the same reason. Paris is just the latest vile act aimed at gaining control. If you knew this maybe it would change your impulse to fight. Or have someone else fight for you."

Again, Agnieszka was speaking directly to Royar. I particularly enjoyed this new suggestion Royar was a coward. That he was an arm-chair general, happy for others to die on his behalf. While Agnieszka's passionate defence bordered on attack, I knew she wasn't defending me. Perhaps she was protecting Mila or maybe this was just an issue she felt strongly about. Whatever the case, Royar was now ready with his answer.

"Now we're getting closer to the truth," Royar said, looking pleased with himself once again.

"You think this is about control? I think you can't compare ancient history with what's happening now."

Royar accented the word 'I' with a forefinger and fist jabbed into his chest. It was a gorilla-like gesture to assert his dominance in the room.

"I'll say it again, people like you, Kevin and Steve are laying out the welcome mat."

Royar pointed the two of us out for good measure.

"If it's a history lesson you want, look up appeasement. Then you'll see what happens when you wait too long before making a military response. You are rolling over and showing your bellies to men with bayonetted rifles who wouldn't think twice about killing you in your bed or killing your family at a sporting event."

Royar was getting more intense but still a long way from losing his cool.

"Funny how it's always men with bayonets and rifles," Kevin said, joining the discussion after Royar pointed him out.

"There's nothing funny about appeasement Kevin. Maybe you'd know that if you had friends in Paris too."

Royar looked emotionally involved for the first time in any discussion.

"I do have friends in Paris Roy." Kevin's tone was conciliatory. "And I am worried for them but that's not why we're here. We could talk about Paris and terrorism all night but we're here for the people in this room, including you."

This was Kevin trying to draw a line under the subject. For his part Royar looked ready to concede. I wondered if he thought a victory on points was just as good as a knockout.

"Let's get back to things we have the power to change before Steve has an aneurism. In any case I want to hear more about Oran's jet-lag."

Kevin's attempted bait-and-switch was complete. I'm sure Royar knew he was being shut down but he decided to let the conversation drop. I imagined he was the sort of person who would keep score and that Agnieszka had now joined Kevin on his hit list. Of course I had already been defeated so I no longer registered any threat.

For his part, Oran accepted Kevin's invitation at face value and found plenty more to say about his flight to Canada and everything he saw when he was there. I wasn't bothered in the slightest that Kevin had just taken control of the session. Or that in Royar's eyes Kevin had just proved he was in charge. Whatever Royar thought I knew this was all part of Kevin's role as a Vet. If Royar's respect for me had to suffer I would find it hard to care less.

• • •

The rest of the session consisted mainly of Oran talking. Royar drifted back to his quad, Agnieszka kept an eye on Mila, and Mila went back to quiet observation and the occasional handwritten note.

As Kevin and I walked home I was still trying to process the evening's events. I may have seemed quiet but I guessed Kevin was used to this by now.

I was thinking to myself how this session wasn't the first time Kevin had stepped in to calm things down. I remembered the first time Kevin and I met. He was already a Vet and could have easily been a group leader although he never wanted this role. I later found out Kevin's experience intimidated some of the leaders he worked with. This had been my knee-jerk reaction too, before I realised having him there was the only way I'd get by.

I warmed to Kevin from the very first day. He'd been the first person to speak to me when I walked into the hall. I must have looked nervous because I wasn't sure I was in the right place. Kevin's welcome immediately put me at ease.

My memories jumped forward a few weeks. A couple of sessions into my grounding programme I was plucking up the courage to share. I knew it had to happen eventually but back then, like I still do today, I get anxious. When I finally shared something I talked round and round in circles.

"Steve expresses himself in ever decreasing spirals of uncertainty and incomprehension," was something my first group leader wrote in her private notes. You get to see your grounding notes when you train to be a group leader. Reading the notes on me was quite a shock.

In that second or third session I remember trying to make a point about being ready to receive help and how important this is. At least it felt important to me at the time. I was just reaching what I thought was a sensible conclusion. Something about not ignoring what's best for me, which I had typically done in the past. When Kevin changed my sharing into a debate.

"Steve, I think the fence you're sitting on is about to collapse," Kevin said.

Most of the group stifled their laughter, including the leader, but Kevin carried on.

"I've only known you a few hours but I'm already fascinated by the way you argue with yourself."

I remember not replying but also not feeling insulted. Even then I knew Kevin had put his finger on one of my character flaws. I was a rambler long before I was a walker.

In the session, Kevin wasn't done with my mini-appraisal.

"If we get to know each other better, which I genuinely hope we do, part of me will love watching these knotted balls of string untangle in your mind, then knot themselves up all over again as you talk. The rest of me just wants to put an end to your suffering. Perhaps with a Taser."

The whole group, me included, laughed out loud at this.

Back in the present I chuckled to myself as we walked along the road.

Kevin has threatened to tase me a couple of times since that meeting. He has also found softer ways to bring me back when I get carried away with my thoughts, or when I'm getting browbeaten by someone like Royar.

Our walk home is almost over so I've wasted the opportunity to chat tonight. Kevin and I have done a lot of our talking on our way home from the hall. I think they've been the times I've enjoyed most.

Although it's only a short walk, on the night Kevin gave me his first appraisal, the two of us stood and talked in the road for over an hour. At one point one of my neighbours came out to see what the noise was.

"Can't you talk at home?" he said.

All I could do was apologise as the unknown neighbour padded back inside in his slippers. His interruption made me lose the thread of our conversation. Kevin just looked at me with a grin.

"You're hilarious Steve. I'll never get tired of listening to you," Kevin said.

I remember him saying it like it was yesterday. I agonised over it for ages before finally accepting he meant it in a good way.

3

"Grounding celebrates the triumph
of humanity over technology.
I want you to embrace every single step."
Elon Mensch

10.40pm
Monday 31 December 2103

FOR THE SECOND year in a row the Community Hall was hosting a New Year's Eve party. This time around I made the effort to go.

It wouldn't be anything like my New Year's Eve experiences from the past but for me that was part of the appeal. I could have easily gone somewhere big tonight. Somewhere like Trafalgar Square, Paris or Princes Street, especially now rail services are running on weekends. But I wanted to be local.

The party itself reminded me of weddings I'd been to where I only knew the bride and groom. Thankfully Kevin stopped by for an hour and the two of us chatted for most of his stay. We avoided talking shop, although we did talk about Agnieszka. The way she stood up to Royar had impressed us both.

"It took guts," Kevin said. "Going toe-to-toe like that with the biggest ego in the room."

I thought about joking with Kevin about who really had the biggest ego but I didn't want my joke to be taken the wrong way.

"Agnieszka was very cool," I said, playing it safe. "Much cooler than me. Royar got me on the back foot and had no problem keeping me there."

Kevin nodded in agreement as I spoke. It didn't happen often but Kevin was preoccupied tonight. Maybe he was still thinking about Agnieszka? I was getting ready to ask him if anything was wrong when an awkward bout of Dad-dancing distracted us both.

"I don't think I've ever seen you dance Steve," Kevin said changing the subject. "Will you be throwing any shapes tonight?"

We both laughed at the mental picture this painted.

"You haven't been paying attention, I danced at Saira's birthday party," I said, pretending to be offended.

"I think that was the last time I danced too," Kevin said in reply.

Perhaps this was why he was uncomfortable. I kicked myself for not realising sooner.

• • •

I didn't stay at the hall long after Kevin left. There was snow on the ground and it was a freezing night so I walked home carefully, watching for ice. The risk of falling made me think about balance. The words stability, poise and equilibrium came to mind, along with images of tightrope walkers and weighing scales.

My thoughts jumped back to the times when I was zipping everywhere. The last thing I could claim about my life back then was balance. For some reason I thought about one of my trips to Rio, where I looked out over the city from what felt like the shoulder of Christ the Redeemer.

"It was a great view but I still felt nothing," I said this out loud to myself.

Unlike my steps, my thoughts started picking up speed. I imagined waterlogged rice fields in Vietnam, although I'd only seen these in photographs. I remembered walking up endless steps to see a Shinto mountain shrine in Japan, and how disappointed I'd been at the end of this climb because my heart only beat faster due to thin air and exertion.

The more I zipped to these spiritual places the less impact they had on me. I'd said this in my introduction to the group in our first session. I reflected again on how this was true.

Nothing had the effect I was looking for back then.

"Why did it take me so long to realise I just needed my feet on the ground?"

I tried to stop thinking about missed opportunities and wasted time. Things hadn't turned out so bad.

Back on the ground I was still walking slowly. The thin snow crackled under my feet. Tiny ice crystals glinted back at me as I looked at the floor. I thought to myself how balance can be such a distraction. In reality we balance without thinking. The idea we can weigh-up different aspects of our life. Measure each side, rearrange and borrow until a perfect state of equilibrium is reached. This is something completely different, another form of dislocation.

"Not to mention impossible," I say into the night air.

There's no satisfaction but my thoughts on balance finish there.

The half-hearted glow of a few early fireworks usher me inside as I reach home.

The house is warm. I make tea and see in the New Year alone.

• • •

7.39pm
Wednesday 2 January 2104
Session 3

With the third session underway I was reflecting on everyone's progress again.

Oran and Agnieszka were already, "on a good landing path," as Elena used to say. Both of them are talking and sharing with growing confidence. They also required the least amount of coaxing from Kevin and me.

Mila is still the quietest participant in the circle but her childhood story had been deeply personal. It takes real courage to share a painful memory like this. My biggest concern for Mila now is her further withdrawal.

"Don't worry, Mila is probably tougher than she looks," I think to myself.

I take a moment to think about Mila's childhood story again. I hope I supported her enough at the time. I make my mind up to support Mila's contributions more actively from now on. It is coming to me for the first time and I don't know what it is, but there is something about Mila that intrigues me.

"Is that intrigues or beguiles Stephen?" says the voice from my id.

The last participant I think about is Royar. Part of me is surprised he keeps turning up. I'm sure it would be easier for Royar to play with his quad somewhere outside of our circle. Royar is still happy distracting himself. Keeping a safe distance from the other participants. I wonder what form of dislocation this is. I also wonder if Royar will find a way to connect with the programme or allow himself to do this. As Mila showed it takes courage.

"Maybe a kind of courage Royar doesn't have," I think to myself.

In my peripheral vision I catch Mila moving which interrupts my train of thought. Mila's whole body appears to tense up. I notice her jaw clenches shut. Her lower cheek ripples along the jawbone as the muscles flex.

There is a pause in the small, Mila takes a deep breath, jerks her head up and speaks.

"I don't know where to start so I'm just going to say it," Mila's voice is surprisingly forceful.

"I lied to you all in our last session. My Mum is still alive and I've never zipped before."

Mila lets go of her breath, trying to release the tension in her body.

I find myself checking around the circle for instant reactions, I notice Mila is doing the same.

Oran had let out a short gasp and was now leaning forward, his hands covering his mouth and nose like a mask. Royar was sitting back, perhaps a little more upright than usual. His head was tilted slightly to one side as he studied Mila with what I guessed was new interest. I imagined Royar seeing Mila in a new light, or perhaps readying some form of showpiece disgust.

I kept looking around the circle as Mila carried on. Whatever excuse she gave us for lying, the hardest part was probably behind her.

"I'm sorry for lying to you all. It was easier to let you think I was normal," Mila said, now looking ashamed.

I recognised the body language well.

"I know all about zipping so it was easy to lie. Everyone knows about zjt. The people, the places, the adventures."

Mila looked down, fiddling with a cord on her jacket. She wound it around her index finger as she spoke.

"I used to write down my favourite zip-travel stories. Then I made up my own. After that it was easier to tell my stories than the truth. No one cared if my stories were true or not."

Mila's confession drifted further into sharing. She carried on talking, all the time looking down.

"I've lived my stories, every single one of them. I even remember new details when I tell them to new people. That's how real they are to me."

A little joy crept in to Mila's voice as she lost herself in the stories once again.

"I know how the flowers smell in Mumbai's botanical gardens. I heard the strange accents of Malaysian forest tribes. I still feel stupid for losing my purse in Boston. I still want to cry even now when I think of my Mum dying of RC."

Mila seemed to shrink even further into her chair.

"But none of it's true."

Now we knew why Mila's childhood story upset her so much. I wanted to tell her not to worry but I stopped myself jumping in. Now wasn't the right time, plus my mind was having a field day with all this new material.

"Are there really forest tribes in Malaysia? What are their accents like?"

I suppressed these thoughts as quickly as I could. I shut my own jaw tight as the idea of asking these ridiculous questions out loud popped into my head.

Everyone had been silent while Mila spoke, even Royar was holding his peace. He must be sensitive enough to realise this was a delicate moment for Mila. I silently credited him for his empathy with Mila's exposed state. Then it dawned on me I was congratulating Royar when I had no idea what he was thinking.

"Thoughts aren't facts Steve," my inner voice reminded me, "When are you going to learn that for good."

The entire circle wanted to hear more of an explanation from Mila. Agnieszka expressed this feeling by softly asking her, "Why?"

Mila replied straight away.

"I'm sorry Agnieszka but I didn't have a choice," Mila blotted her eyes with a tissue as she spoke.

She looked Agnieszka in the eye. Mila was ashamed but she was no longer scared to look us all in the eye.

"All I did was tell a story. If I told you the truth there would be nothing to tell," Mila said, perhaps realising the truth was inevitable now she had referred to it out loud.

I felt for Mila but I'd also seen this before. She wasn't the first person to think her life was insignificant. To believe she didn't have a story worth telling. I'd heard stories from other participants who felt this way. I'd felt it more than once too. It took me a long time to learn that people who think they are nothing always have one thing in common.

"They're wrong," I remind myself.

I know this now. Mila will know it one day too, and it will make her feel better. She'll know everyone has a true story, and every true story deserves to be told. We just have to give ourselves permission and the journey time to see it for what it is. No better, no worse than a true story from anyone else.

"Maybe Mila will get there tonight?" I asked myself, this was my hope for her at least.

Mila gathered herself before sharing the truth.

"My Mum took me to work with her every day, before and after school. She kept house for twelve families in the gated estate up the road."

Mila's voice told us this was no longer an apology.

"Most of the houses were empty. We'd rotate our way through them, keeping food and flowers fresh. We handled deliveries, zipped clothes and all kinds of stuff to their owners around the world. There are sweatshirts with more grid time than me."

Mila was the only one to laugh at this.

"We talked to the families all the time. I talked to the kids about their trips, where they went and what happened. I liked their stories so I wrote them down. Mum never had much interest in travel and I was too young to zip on my own. I never had anyone to visit anyway."

The group was silent as Mila carried on.

"When the shutdown happened most of our families were at their other homes. They asked Mum to keep their houses going. No one thought the grid would be down for long."

By now, most of the group had breathed out. I was usually the only one to notice when people were holding their breath. At some stage we'd all been doing this while Mila spoke.

"Maybe you're wondering why someone who never zipped before needs to be grounded? It doesn't matter if I've never been to these places. These stories are part of my life. My best memories are in some of these places," Mila said, the hope in her voice implored us to understand.

I found Mila's dislocation very easy to recognise. Her true story made perfect sense to me.

"Maybe the shutdown hasn't changed my life. I wasn't travelling before and I'm not travelling now but I know the difference. No grid means no more zip-travel stories. Without them I don't know who or where I am."

The pain Mila felt looked real enough. I imagined a growing sympathy for her around the room. It was quite a turn-around from where Mila had started out with her confession. I wondered if a change of mood like this could have been foreseen.

"Nope, you couldn't make this stuff up," was the answer I kept to myself.

While I was thinking, Mila talked about signing up to Journey Time.

"I wanted to see if grounding could bring me back to reality, instead of a life lived in these stories."

Mila raised her quad as she spoke.

"I hoped... I still hope grounding will mean living my life for real. I know it sounds stupid but without my stories I wouldn't be me. Before I came here tonight, throwing them away felt like erasing myself. Without them my life was nothing."

I decided now was the right time to give Mila some support.

I started by saying Mila wasn't the only one who found her own ways to cope. As someone who suffers from dislocation I know the syndrome has many forms. I told Mila how surprised I'd been when I learned about people and communities all over the world who had never been on the grid. How despite this, their lives were full of travel and dreams of places they'd never been.

I stopped myself talking about Australian aboriginal <u>dreamtime</u>, although this was where I desperately wanted to go. I searched for a non-mystical example instead and ended up talking about fiction and the escape storytelling creates.

"You clearly have a talent for story," I say to Mila.

Then I fail to stop myself wandering off on this tangent. I talk about Jonathan Swift, how he sent Lemuel Gulliver around the world and back again, all from the tip of his pen. I can see the odd looks around the room. It's not like me but I decide to ignore them.

"Mila, you have a gift. A gift I believe is perfectly adjusted to our time. Now more than ever the world needs its storytellers and the world's storytellers need to be grounded."

I thought this was safer territory but looking around the circle not everyone agreed. I still wasn't worried because my message appeared to hit home with Mila and that was all I cared about in this moment. Mila gave me a little smile to confirm this. I thanked her as enthusiastically as I knew how, for having the courage to share, and I meant every word.

The group chimed in with their own form of acknowledgement when Agnieszka told us all about lying to her boss about climbing Sydney Harbour Bridge.

"When he asked if I had any photos, I just downloaded someone's holiday snaps from the internet," Agnieszka said with a reassuring smile.

Everyone laughed at this. Mila looked much better, almost content.

With the laughter fading Agnieszka turned to me.

"You never did get around to telling us your childhood story Steve."

Agnieszka said this with a mischievous look on her face.

"Everyone else has had their turn except you," she added.

"You're right Agnieszka, I've had long enough to think. Mila has been twice, I've lost count of Oran's stories. I promise to tell you my story in the next session, I'll even go first if you like?" I said, surprising myself at how confident this sounded.

"Sounds good to me," Agnieszka said in reply. "I won't let you get away with it a second time."

I had no doubt Agnieszka was right.

• • •

"So how was that for you?" Kevin got his question in first on our way home.

I thought for a moment before answering.

"I'd say it was a good session. My highlight was definitely Mila. The girls are really showing the way when it comes to sharing."

I hoped this didn't sound sexist but feared it probably did.

"That took real backbone," Kevin agreed. "Mila and Agnieszka are both something else."

Kevin looked pleased with himself.

"Although Agnieszka's still your favourite," I said, taking my lead from his voice.

I was pleased to hear Kevin laugh out loud, I didn't tease him back all that often.

"Oh dear. If you've noticed I'm not being very subtle," Kevin said, still smiling.

His hands were buried into his jacket pockets, making his shoulders hunch forward. The combination of this and the subject of Agnieszka made Kevin look vulnerable, if only for a second.

"It's never happened to me before but I like her, Agnieszka I mean."

I knew who Kevin meant, I just think he likes saying her name.

"She's smart and she has this way of dealing with things. Take the last two sessions. Agnieszka comforted Mila when she thought she was upset about her Mum. When she found out that was a lie Agnieszka could have given Mila hell or cut her off."

Kevin turned to look at me as he spoke.

"You and I have seen this stuff before but for all I know Agnieszka was seeing it for the first time and she handled it beautifully. Straight in with support, the first to fess up with a lie of her own."

For the first time I realised Kevin was taken. There wasn't much doubt before but this latest exchange made it obvious between us. Kevin liked Agnieszka, which was something of a breakthrough for him.

I cleared my throat, pretending I was about to say something important.

"Of course as group leader I feel obliged to remind you of JT's rules on fraternisation with participants," I said, doing my best imitation of a pencil-pushing voice.

Kevin laughed again.

"That voice suits you Steve. You make a very convincing petty official, I think you missed your vocation."

I thought about giving Kevin a friendly pat on the back as we parted but I usually got that kind of gesture wrong. When I've tried it before people wonder what I'm doing, like I'm putting a sticker on their back or something just as juvenile. Maybe they pick up on my unease and this makes them suspicious. I remind myself all of this could just be in my mind.

Pausing to think kills the moment for a pat on the back. I resign myself to the fact that spontaneous physical gestures will never be my thing.

"Go to bed Steve, before you think yourself to death," Kevin said, clapping me on the shoulder as he spoke and finally waking me from my thoughts.

4

"My secret to success?
Never lose heart."
Elon Mensch

7.05am <u>EST</u>
Wednesday 16 January 2104

ELON MENSCH SAT on the edge of his desk, taking in a bird's-eye view of New York.

From this office he could see Manhattan in every direction but this was his favourite by far.

Elon studied it all over again. The great valley looking north up Park Avenue, the river of people on the boulevard itself, the glowing peak of the Chrysler Building in his peripheral vision to the right.

All this was usually behind him.

"It needs to be at my back," Elon said during the re-design of the building, "or I'll get nothing done."

Elon Mensch was tall, athletic and in his late forties. From 50 yards he looked like the perfect physical specimen.

"That's close enough," was one of his recent lines to the pack of paparazzi videographers who recorded his every move, "Only Mrs. Mensch gets a close-up with her breakfast."

Like all great business success stories Elon came out of nowhere, or 'Nowhere, Illinois' as he liked to say. In his early life there had been no advantages, no breeding of note, no schooling of any repute. But he didn't hide any of this. It was all on record, put there by Elon himself with his pithy one-liners and by wearing his 'soul-on-his-sleeve' as one biographer put it. It wasn't a surprise that Elon was widely admired. Even his harshest critics took care diluting their bile.

Elon thanked his humble beginnings publicly all the time, most often in his work with challenging students in struggling schools. He also thanked his lineage for his statesman-like bearing, although in Elon's case this was perhaps the least of his gifts. Now at the height of his power, the vast majority of people saw Elon as one of the greatest entrepreneurs, business visionaries, philanthropists and communicators of his generation.

Not that his global reputation was concerning him right now.

Right now Elon was engrossed. This view behind his desk had a strange effect on him. In this moment it was making him think about dissonance.

Although it only really came home to him here, in every one of his flagship office suites, Elon felt separated. He thought about distance again.

Disconnection, dislocation, discordance, divorce. Elon was trying to capture what he felt and what he saw.

The world writhed in silence on the other side of the seven-millimetre sapphire glass. This is what made Elon uncomfortable. Not the writhing or the seething, just the fact he wasn't part of it.

• • •

Today was nothing special in Elon's routine.

Right on schedule he got up at 5am for the Euro-African and overnight news briefings. Following this was an hour of Iyengar Yoga in the gym. Then a breakfast of steamed fish and rice, a baby aspirin, statin tablet and a cup of green tea. All this preceded a short walk to the JT central hub in Midtown.

Seventeen appointments made up Elon's diary for the day. A mix of strategy briefings, media interviews, updates on operational projects and ongoing organisation-change programmes. Keeping pace with JT's rapid expansion was almost a full-time job.

Booked in for 3.30pm was Elon's regular break from the back-to-back meetings. Fifteen minutes of meditation, which in the days of zip-travel he took in the location of his choice. Directly after this at 3.50pm was Elon's grounding half-hour. His office kept a master schedule for all JT activity worldwide. Every day a grounding group was picked for him to join. To ensure equal representation across regions, the only non-random selection element was longitude. Today's group would be selected from those in countries intersected by the 0° meridian.

The group half-hour was the daily event Elon looked forward to more than anything else.

It was the only appointment in his diary with the grace to overrun.

• • •

7.10pm
Wednesday 16 January 2104
Session 4

I made it to the hall earlier than usual and wasn't at all surprised to see Agnieszka arrive first.

"Hi Steve, don't forget you owe me one childhood story," she said, the pretend scorn on her face breaking into a grin.

I thought about Kevin's confession. It wasn't hard to see why he liked Agnieszka. She was complicated but not at all hardened or bitter. In truth she was the opposite, welcoming and sweet, but Agnieszka could also look after herself whatever company she found herself in. We'd all seen the evidence of that.

Agnieszka also made it her business to look out for other people. I remembered her childhood story and her mother's advice. I thought again how smart she must have been at such a young age to realise her Mum was right.

With the two of us alone in the hall it seemed a good time to ask Agnieszka about something else that had been on my mind. Kevin had given Agnieszka a nickname and I wanted to make sure she was okay with this. Kevin gave everyone nicknames. In this case it was really none of my business but I couldn't help being curious.

"Agnieszka, do you mind if I ask why Kevin calls you Alice?" I said.

"Of course I don't mind," Agnieszka said smiling, "Kevin and I were chatting about life after ZJT. I said to him, 'Sometimes I think I've woken up the wrong side of the looking glass'. Kevin immediately replied, 'That's it! I'm calling you Alice.' The moment he said it I knew it was perfect for me."

I satisfied myself Agnieszka was more than comfortable talking about this, which was good because I wanted to know more.

"Is it perfect because we live in Wonderland?" I asked Agnieszka, although I wasn't quite sure if the question made sense.

"No, it's perfect because I've always loved Alice," Agnieszka said in a straightforward reply.

She took a second or two longer to think about her answer.

"Kevin couldn't have known it but Alice has always been a hero of mine. In a fairy-tale world she had the most powerful magic."

Agnieszka gave me a knowing smile.

"Innocence," she said.

"I had no idea," was all I managed to say before Agnieszka shared more.

"In the real world, Alice wouldn't stand for any nonsense or abuse. She's the sort of person who would fight injustice. Question powerful people without fear. My Alice would put flowers down gun barrels, stare down them if need be. An Anne Frank, Malala Yousafzai or Sophie Scholl, that's who she would be."

The more Agnieszka spoke, the more convincing she became.

"Alice is also a feminist icon. A turning point for women's movements everywhere. Some people think Lewis Carroll was a genius, others think he was an opium fiend with a little-girl fixation. I don't care what he was, Lewis Carroll gave us Alice and if Kevin sees Alice in me, I'm happy with that."

Agnieszka spoke in such an effortless way. If I didn't know better I'd say she didn't care but of course the opposite was true. This was all so personal to her. So much thought had gone into it. Agnieszka had spoken this way when she talked about her Mother. No argument, no doubt, just pure connection.

I thought it best to say something before my thoughts about Agnieszka carried me away.

"I hope you didn't mind me asking?" I said, realising she had already answered this question before.

"Not at all Steve, and feel free to call me Alice too," Agnieszka said smiling broadly, maybe teasing me a little.

"I'm not sure if that would be appropriate," I said without thinking.

"Agnieszka's still fine if you don't approve," she said in quick reply.

"She even has the same sense of humour as Kevin," I thought to myself, "I reckon they've both met their match."

● ● ●

The rest of the group had drifted in while Alice and I were talking.

Kevin had been chatting with Oran. Royar and Mila were already sitting in the circle. Alice and I joined them and we got the session underway.

I decided to offer my childhood story immediately. The group accepted so I started reading from my quad.

"My friend Gavin came over one day. We would have been about eight or nine at the time."

My plan was to make a confident start.

"It was summer and were playing in the garden, pretending to be Sherlock Holmes with his magnifying glass. Yes Kevin, I was a geek even then."

I noticed there was genuine laughter around the circle at this.

"It was a hot day and we used the glass to magnify the sun's rays. Gavin told me the beam of light could make an ant explode. I found some ants and put this to the test."

I started to feel uncomfortable because I knew where the story was going.

"When the spot of white light hits an ant it starts to wobble. Then there's a tiny wisp of smoke, then the ant disappears. I honestly can't remember if it explodes or not."

No one is laughing any more.

"Gavin got bored after the second ant but I was fascinated and kept looking for more. Years later I read that serial killers often start out with cruelty to animals. I never went on to kill anything bigger than an ant, but I worried about being a serial killer for years."

It didn't sound bad when I typed it but I'm now realising this wasn't the best story I could have told.

"Jesus Steve," Kevin said to me in a low hiss.

The smile was back on Royar's face. Oran looked disturbed, staring at me past a slightly wrinkled nose.

Mila asked me a direct question.

"What did you learn Steve?" she said. "Wasn't that the whole point of telling this story?"

Mila's question was genuine, although I thought the lesson was obvious. I did a stupid thing as a kid and it taught me something. It taught me I used to get too wrapped up in stuff to realise I might be harming someone or something else. I didn't want to kill the ants. I didn't really mean to harm them. The whole thing just fascinated me and I got carried away.

But none of this was obvious.

So far the explanation was all in my mind. As far as the people in the room were concerned I'd just confessed to being a junior psychopath.

I tried to explain myself and put things right.

"If it makes a difference, the next thing I did was hold the magnifying glass over my own hand. The spot of light appeared on my skin. I watched it for a second then I felt the searing pain. That's when I realised what I had done to the ants," I looked at Mila as I spoke.

"Too little too late, I know that now," I said, hoping she wouldn't be disgusted.

More than anything else, I found myself worrying about what Mila thought of me.

She thought for a moment before replying.

"You're not a serial killer Steve, you were just a dumb kid," Mila said, shrugging her shoulders.

I don't think anyone has ever called me dumb with so much kindness before.

The tension seemed to melt from the room, or perhaps it was just my relief at Mila's forgiveness.

"You should have been a scientist Steve," Agnieszka said, joining the discussion.

"Although with your methods, by now you'd either be dead or struck off."

Agnieszka joined Mila in making me feel better. Her light-hearted support was another encouraging sign.

"Thanks Alice," I said, "I hope my story was worth the wait."

In reality I just hoped my story would erase itself from everyone's mind.

I also realised I'd now have to explain to the whole group why I'd just called Agnieszka Alice.

• • •

With my disaster of a story and Alice's new name out of the way, the group found a good rhythm of sharing and reflection. Oran and Mila had been using their journals regularly and had plenty to contribute. Despite the embarrassing start, I felt like we were getting close to an important tipping point in the programme. The leadership role Kevin and I had to play was slowly changing from teasing out input, to managing its flow.

Sharing always flows more freely when people trust each other, although perhaps the most important factor is individuals learning to trust themselves. The handbook talks about this extensively. How trust spreads around JT circles like a positive virus. Kevin had been working in sessions long enough to recognise the point we were nearing. It was an important shift in any programme but it was by no means a one-way street. Things can easily go backwards so it was still our job to manage with care.

The remainder of the first half seemed to go by in a flash, which was another good sign. We took a break for coffee, although it was the kind of break where the conversation keeps rolling. Oran was his usual talkative self. This time he was sharing new rumours about the grid. I think he liked to be seen as an insider on the subject. He definitely liked to be the centre of attention whenever that was possible. Royar was particularly interested in Oran's zjt news and more than once questioned him down to technical details. I was impressed to see Oran handle this well.

Before long the break was over and we were all back in the circle for part two. About twenty-minutes in, and in the middle of Mila sharing some recent reflections, my quad sounded with a loud ringing tone. I cursed myself as the noise halted Mila mid-sentence. She was so much more comfortable talking to the group but this wouldn't help. A ringing quad is distracting enough when it happens to a participant, for a group leader it's a cardinal sin.

I felt my cheeks redden as I struggled to get the device out of my pocket. The incoming call sound was now confusing me because I always set my device to silent before every session. It's part of my routine and I've never forgotten to do it, not even once.

An even more unsettling thought leapt into my mind. There were only three entries in my contacts whose notifications were set to override privacy. Becoming even more flustered as the device sounded again, I finally wrestled it from my pocket.

I recognised the flashing insignia immediately and flipped open the receiver to activate the call.

"Hello Mr Morrish, this is Mr Mensch's office," a cultured voice intoned.

"Please unfold your quad to tablet and stand by for Mr Mensch to join your session in one minute's time."

"This can't be real," I thought to myself.

One minute was all I had to tell the group what was going on.

5

"The first question I ask in any business situation,
How big is your boat?"
Elon Mensch

**8.49pm (3.49pm EST)
Wednesday 16 January 2104**

EVERYONE WAS STUNNED. Even Kevin looked surprised.

You could attend hundreds, maybe even thousands of JT sessions and not be selected in this way. Someone with a better understanding of maths could work out the probability. I immediately gave up trying to calculate in order to come to terms with the fact this was happening to us, and it was happening right now.

I tried my best to make the next fifty-five seconds count.

"This might sound unlikely but in less than a minute Elon Mensch is joining us live through my quad."

A short explanation was never going to be enough but I wanted to break the news up front rather than soften the blow. At least people would have time to ask questions this way.

Kevin was already explaining to Oran how everyone at JT knows Elon joins one group per day.

Royar asked why he hadn't been warned this might happen at the beginning of the programme.

"Surely it's a selling point?" he said.

I answered Royar by telling him the odds are so small we're given no special warning or preparation. I personally think Royar was annoyed because he hadn't worn his favourite suit.

Anticipation around the circle was rising. My excitement was rising too. I still found it hard to believe we'd been chosen. You could go through an entire JT career and not get this call.

I exchanged a quick glance with Kevin. Both of us knew we'd answered as many questions as we could in the available time. Everyone's attention was now drawn to the on-screen timer as the last few seconds ticked down. I'd fixed the tablet's steadymount to the back of a hastily added chair and watched as the screen changed from the familiar JT logo to Elon's equally familiar face.

"Hello Everyone. Hello Agnieska, Kevin, Mila, Oran, Royar and Steve."

The quad's intelligent camera allowed Elon to look around the room as he spoke.

Everyone was quiet.

"I'm Elon Mensch. For anyone who doesn't know, I'm Steve and Kevin's boss, so get ready to see their best behaviour."

The group looked between Kevin, Elon and me. Royar sat forward in his chair, I could be wrong but he seemed to make what looked like a fist-pump.

"Before you tell me how badly your group leaders are doing, you should know I'm not here to check up on them or anyone else."

Elon continued his smooth-as-glass flow. I silently wished I could be half as comfortable addressing a group.

"Steve, Kevin, I'm not here to take over. I'm here as a participant and I want you all to keep sharing exactly as you were. All I ask is to be included, the same way you would include any new member into the group."

Elon smiled as he spoke. It could easily sound false but I knew Elon wanted to be treated like a regular participant. Looking around the circle I think the others were buying his sincerity too.

A short pause by Elon made this a good time for either Kevin or me to respond. As usual I was thinking instead of picking up my cue.

"Thank you Elon," Kevin said, there was hardly any variation in his tone. "To bring you up to speed on tonight's session, Steve has told an unsettling childhood story, Agnieszka is now called Alice and Royar was in the middle of telling us how disappointed he is with the whole grounding experience."

Kevin had a twinkle in his eye the quad's camera probably couldn't see. Both Royar and I were mortified, perhaps Royar more so because he'd said nothing of the sort.

Royar shifted uncomfortably in his chair. He was doing his best to look cool in front of this powerful new presence. Despite his feelings about JT, Royar understood executive power. He knew better than anyone that there was a new 500lb gorilla in the room.

For the time being at least, Royar's chest beating was over. Under the circumstances I thought his reply to Elon was quite composed.

"I'm glad you joined us Mr. Mensch. Your personal commitment to JT customers is impressive. Congratulations on finding a place in your business for a team leader with sociopathic tendencies like Steve, and a Vet with a bizarre sense of humour like Kevin."

Royar's response was a master-class in passive-aggressive creepery. I know it's unprofessional but I despised him all over again.

"Please Royar, call me Elon," was the initial reply. "I'm glad you like our team leaders and that you've understood my joining you is a customer thing, but I must correct you on one point. I don't join groups for the benefit of our customers, I do it for me."

Watching Elon wave away a corporate shit-fly like Royar helped my anger fade.

"My first JT experience was as a participant just like you. Same as everyone else who comes through our doors. Everything JT is today can be traced back to a circle same as the one we're sitting in right now."

Elon's response was a study of confidence and calm. Royar's challenges were being ignored. Maybe Elon had figured Royar out. But how could he ignore the fact a customer just called me a sociopath. At the very least I was now expecting a call from central HR later this evening. While everyone else was cool, my paranoia rose and I started to sweat.

Royar wasn't getting things his way but he was sharp enough to have a reply.

"That's impressive Elon. I was expecting a response about Kevin and Steve but now I think about it, what you said is actually more interesting. Do you really keep up with the grounding programme yourself?" Royar said.

"Now we all know what a genuinely interested question from Royar sounds like," I thought to myself as Elon replied.

"Absolutely Roy, do you mind if I call you Roy?" Elon said.

Royar raised his palms to gesture that he didn't mind, not that Elon was waiting for his approval.

"If I didn't have absolute belief in what our groups are doing, if I can't take part and find this conversation believable, then something is deeply wrong with my position as JT CEO."

Elon shared more insight into his thinking.

"If there's more we can learn, I want to be out there looking and listening for it. Any less would be dereliction of my duty to the firm," Elon said.

I tried to end my HR worries by focusing on Elon instead. I realised that despite all the coverage I'd only ever seen him in pre-recorded form before. This transmission was live, plus the intimacy of a small audience added a completely new dimension. If I was going to be sacked later on, I couldn't think of a better way to go.

Elon spoke again, popping the bubble of my thoughts.

"So what's next Steve?" he said directly to me.

Elon looked at me through the screen. I wondered what he saw. Was he thinking about Royar's comment? Did he think I hadn't been listening? I tried to clear my mind and did my best to respond.

"Well Elon, I. I mean we. We've all… That's to say Kevin and I have been. Sorry…"

"You're dropping the ball Steve," Elena used to say to me at times like this.

Her voice in my ear wasn't comforting me now.

It was all in my mind but Royar was getting in the way. I couldn't stop thinking about his comment and the look on his face, a look of pure enjoyment right now.

"Elon will think I'm a nutcase," I think to myself.

In reality I must look ridiculous.

"Take it easy Steve, I know you're nervous," I hear Elon say to me.

Again, his voice was cool.

"Take your time," Elon carried on speaking to me.

I drew a deeper breath, making sure not to catch Royar's eye.

"Whenever you're ready, just tell me what you and the group have been doing," Elon said, again it sounded soothing.

"Just tell me what you have been doing," Elon's words repeated themselves in my mind.

Somehow Elon had made this sound possible.

I closed my eyes and re-composed myself again.

"I don't want my mistakes to define who I am. I don't want people like Royar to affect me this way. I want to do a good job. I want Elon to know he can trust me. I'm not a serial killer."

I think all of this and more to myself.

I tighten my stomach muscles as hard as I can, then I let the tension go.

"Do what the man said," I think to myself. "Tell him what we've been doing. Take it slow."

Deliberately avoiding everyone's gaze, I open my eyes and start talking.

"Thank you Elon," I say, with a slight break in my voice.

"We started with introductions."

I start as simply as I know how, then I reach for the handbook to find my feet.

"Everyone has shared a personal story. When someone new joins, we ask them to do the same."

I knew this was the right procedure. Remembering this makes me feel better, if only by a degree.

"Only when the new participant is happy and ready to share of course," I say to Elon, allowing myself to look directly at his screen.

It is almost a direct quote from the handbook he wrote.

"Perfect," Elon replied. "Great job Steve. And yes, I am happy and ready to share."

My relief is immense.

Elon will share and I will get more recovery time, starting right now.

"I'm Elon Mensch, and like Steve and Kevin, I also work for Journey Time," Elon recapped.

"In the past I would have made a point of joining you in person but today that journey would take too long, so please don't take my virtual appearance personally. The grid being down is still something we're all adjusting to."

Elon already had us all transfixed. The resolution and quality of his picture was so good I found myself picking out Manhattan landmarks behind him. I thought to myself how holding an audience's attention was a kind of magic. I welcomed all of these benign thoughts as Elon continued his intro.

"Zip-travel and I had a very close relationship. Right up to the last few hours before the grid went down I was still zipping. That surprises some people, given the company I work for, but I never saw the contradiction. I work for a global organisation, more than one in fact. Zip-travel allowed me to see more of my customers, my organisation and its people."

Elon's intro was taking on a more reflective quality.

"I had plenty of struggles with dislocation, so it wasn't always easy. I didn't struggle too much with places the way some people do. My dislocation was feeling removed from other people. The only distance I agonised over was the distance I felt from people like you."

As an admission this could have sounded insincere but Elon's sharing was effortless. In saying this I'm probably overlooking years of exhausting emotional investment, but talking from the heart seemed to come naturally to him.

"When the grid went down it created a huge gap in my life. Massive gaps between me and the people I was closest to. At first I couldn't see how my life would function in this new world. The irony of my situation was crushing, 'Mr Journey Time' floored by his dependence on zjt."

There was no doubt this was ironic. At the time Elon's critics had a field day, although I never considered it from his perspective. This was the first time I thought of him as a normal guy and not a superstar, super-famous CEO.

"It was painful at first but I realised very quickly this was the right way for me to feel."

Elon went deeper into his sharing.

"Letting people know I was struggling was the right way for me to respond, as a person and in my professional position. If the shutdown didn't hurt me, what business did I have in an organisation like JT? What could I possibly know of the lives we support?"

This statement hit home with everyone around the circle but it was Elon's humility that carried it through. He was sharing something real with us, person-to-person, as an equal. I was sure everyone felt the same way.

"Maybe I knew what the pain felt like before the grid went down. As a ZJT-d sufferer I knew the technology could hurt me. That original hurt started my relationship with JT in the first place. I walked through the door of a local group just like this. I started talking, and I started rebuilding my life."

Elon's eye contact around the group was masterful. A perfect balance of honest and inclusive. For the first time since dropping the ball a few minutes ago, I allowed myself to look around the circle. The belief they were hearing something important for the first time was written on everyone's face.

Elon went on with his story.

"JT was still small back then but I knew it was special because of the people I met and the impact that early version of the programme had on me. I knew JT would be huge. Hugely profitable for sure but also huge because it deserved to touch so many more lives than it ever could back then."

Elon paused, checking we were all still with him. I got the impression he wouldn't share like this with just anyone. It made me feel special.

"Some big things have happened since then. I got more and more involved with JT and watched the organisation grow. Then we all felt the hammer of RC fall. I felt this personally too."

Elon looked away from the camera for what felt like the first time since he joined the group. I guessed he'd lost someone close.

He was almost instantly back on track.

"Some markets and biographers call me a genius. People who don't like me call me plenty of other names too. I'll happily admit to anyone that I am none of these things. There's nothing special or different about me. All I did, all I ever do, is react to events."

Elon fixed his gaze into the lens once again.

"All I ever do is weigh up my options and choose the only one I can live with. In JT's case the only other choice I ever had was to turn people away. That was never a choice I was going to make."

Elon had reached a new jumping off point in his sharing. He probably guessed we would listen to him speak for as long as he wanted but he also knew time was short and that progress was all about mutual sharing.

"If that works for you as an introduction Steve, do you mind if I ask what's next on the agenda?"

A wave of nods rolled around the room. I responded to my cue much better this time around.

"Well Elon, we've recently shared childhood stories. As the new member of our group, my next step would be to ask for yours," I said.

I realised this was asking Elon to follow on with more sharing. But this was also genuinely what I'd ask from any new group member at this point.

Elon was quick with his reply.

"I've done most of the talking but maybe I can see the need to do a little more. I could say I'm not ready to share again, but that wouldn't be true. Instead I'll be quick, but only because the perfect story has just come to mind."

Once again Elon's face conveyed sincerity, along with mischevious deep thought.

"I don't think I've ever shared this one in a group session before," Elon said, before launching into a new round of sharing.

"I've kept it to myself before now but the first question I ask in any business situation is always, 'How big is your boat?' I appreciate it doesn't make much sense without the back-story."

Elon beamed a smile that wasn't entirely for our benefit. He was enjoying himself now.

"One Summer, my family and I stayed with friends on the coast. I was looking forward to this vacation for months and planned to spend all my time on the beach. Day one was perfect. On day two I was walking past a boatyard on my way to the sea, when a voice called out, 'Hey Kid, How'd you like to earn fifty bucks? All you have to do is sand down my boat.'"

Elon imitated a gruff, salty sounding voice.

"I looked round and saw a guy stood beside a small wooden rowboat. My weekly allowance was five dollars back then, so for fifty dollars I said yes straight away. I spent every day of the next three weeks sanding down the hull of a thirty-foot yacht."

For a second Elon looked miffed all over again, then he told us his response.

"Before every business decision I ever made since, I have thought about that boat. Sanding that boat reminds me money will never matter more than my time. This helps as a reminder too," Elon said.

He raised his left hand to the camera, pulled down the cuff of his shirt an inch or two, and turned his arm so the inside of his wrist could be seen. A small italic tattoo displayed the equation, '$v = \$ \div t$'.

A new smile crept on to Elon's face. I thought he looked almost fatherly this time.

"Since that day I never said yes to anything before doing this calculation, and finding out the size of the other guy's boat."

Elon's story had an instant effect on the group. People were visibly lifted by what they had seen. There was no doubt Elon was still an extraordinary figure in everyone's eyes but he'd also let us see him as a powerless little boy. In his own words, Elon told us how someone slicker outfoxed him, but he learned from the experience. Not many people are prepared to look vulnerable. Even fewer people in Elon's position would willingly disempower themselves by making that choice. It instantly made sense why Elon was where he was. Why he was so successful. How someone like him could see the potential in grounding and build it into the greatest business success of our time.

I imagined similar thoughts going through other people's minds. Royar was furiously writing notes on his quad. Kevin was sitting back with a smile on his face. Alice was also smiling, although a disbelieving shake of the head revealed more of her feelings.

We had just heard an incredible story.

Mila and Oran looked even more awestruck than me. The two of them were leaning forward gazing into the screen. On the screen itself, Elon looked like a craftsman standing back to admire a masterpiece he'd just completed, but there was also humility on his face. He was satisfied for sure but the impact of his work was surprising him again. It was almost as if he wasn't sure why it touched other people as deeply as it did.

I thought how tricky it was going to be for me to move things on but Elon did this for me, first by asking Kevin and I for permission, then by taking a series of questions from the group.

I sat back hoping to ask a question myself but I knew there wouldn't be enough time. I wanted to ask Elon about more of the things he had seen, and to ask more about his battles with ZJT-d. I also wanted to find out what he thought was going to happen in the future. I satisfied myself that one or two of his answers touched on these areas as he chatted with the group. Taking a back seat was also the right thing for me to do.

Before any of us were ready it was time for Elon to sign off. Once again I thought he did this with effortless grace, in a way that made everyone feel like the last hour was the highlight of his day.

Elon thanked us for letting him disrupt our session. He thanked Kevin and me for being what he called, "JT's beating heart." Then he thanked our participants for being, "the reason JT is still here," making sure they appreciated their connection with everyone who had grounded before them.

With a wave, this time from his right hand, Elon was gone.

The screen of my quad briefly went blank before fading back up with the familiar JT logo.

• • •

We spent so long wrapping the session up Kevin and I almost had to shoo people out of the hall. The conversations even continued while I locked the doors and as we walked through the car park to the road.

When people finally left, there were affectionate waves as they went their separate ways. Incredulous shakes of the head were still going on all round. Smiles were everywhere.

For a moment I wished Arle had stuck around to be part of this. I hoped her Father would never get to hear what she had missed, or that he wouldn't be heartless enough to blame her if he did.

On our way home Kevin and I were walking on air.

"The two faces I will never forget are yours when that call came in, and Royar's when he realised what I said to Elon."

Kevin was in his element.

Despite my ill-judged story and my embarrassment in front of Elon, this had been a good day for us both. Just like Kevin, everyone would have their own story about today. We would all have our own reasons and our own relationship with this event. The one constant throughout would be Elon Mensch and the way he made us fall in love with JT and grounding all over again.

6

"Nothing kills group sharing
like a samba-class at the door."
Elon Mensch

**8.22pm
Wednesday 30 January 2104
Session 5**

WE WERE ALL still on a high after Elon's appearance in the last
session.

Oran had messaged his family and friends the night it happened. He
told us how jealous they all were and how a few friends had even signed
up to JT in the hope of meeting Elon too. Oran thought this was hilarious.

Mila was still quite star-struck. I asked her if this had anything to
do with the force of Elon's personality. She thought about this for a
moment then said no. The thing that impressed her more than anything else was the way Elon revealed himself.

"He just spoke like he had nothing to hide," Mila said.

Alice had been impressed by Elon's personal commitment to
grounding. She explained how she used to think Elon supported
the programme out of necessity, but hearing him talk about his
experiences in person had changed her view on this. There was no

doubt in her mind Elon's relationship with JT began with grounding and continues to have grounding at its heart.

Royar was the most wary with his reactions but even he admitted Elon's personal presence went way beyond his expectations.

"I've met plenty of CEOs before," Royar said, "But he was by far the most convincing."

Our conversation about Elon turned into extended discussions on grounding, partly thanks to Elon's admission that grounding had to help him before he realised how much it could help anyone else. This led to a mini-speech from Royar on the subject of self-interest, where he used Elon's example to tell us how even the most unselfish acts can be selfishly motivated.

"I want what's best for other people but I also want what's best for me," Royar said at one point.

As Royar spoke Mila imitated him by feigning disinterest and button-mashing the screen of her quad. As well as being funny it was great to see Mila do this. It was a sure sign she was becoming comfortable in the circle.

"And a sure sign you are watching her," my uninhibited thoughts pointed out.

For his part Royar was too busy talking to notice.

"What's best for me isn't necessarily bad for someone else. The two things aren't always opposed," Royar said, finishing his speech for now.

Alice was the first to respond.

"Come on Royar, that's just something selfish people say. Why don't you just admit you always put yourself first?" she said.

There was a hint of hostility in her voice. Alice's original argument with Royar felt like it was from another time but I remember it well. Despite Alice saying she disliked playing devil's advocate, she had no problem being provocative.

"I'm not rising to your bait Alice," Royar said with a smile. "I'm just saying individualism and self-interest aren't the same thing. There are plenty of things I can do that are good for me, and good for other people too. Grounding is a perfect example."

Royar pointed at Kevin and me as he spoke.

"These two helped themselves with the programme, now they help other people. I'm yet to be convinced how much they're helping but that's another story."

I ignored the latest jab in our direction, this was just Royar having fun.

"I hear what you're saying Roy but I think you're looking down the telescope the wrong way," Alice said to Royar in reply.

"Think more broadly for a moment," Alice continued, "What about the greater good? What about altruism? What about sacrifice? All these good things happen because some people choose to put others first. Where would we be as a society if everyone was just selfish?"

This exchange between Royar and Alice had started mildly enough but it was inching closer to the heart, especially for Alice.

"A brave try Alice," Royar said with a dismissive wave. "But your greater good is just individual good multiplied a thousand or a million times."

I would have liked more time to think about this but Royar wasn't waiting for anyone to catch up.

"Altruism and self-interest are two sides of the same coin."

Royar spoke directly to Alice again.

"You wouldn't be here if you really believed in greater good anyway. You'd be out there doing charity work or trying to get the grid switched back on. Show me an altruist and I'll show you an enlightened individualist every time."

Royar looked delighted with the way this parting shot came out.

Now I'd caught up with the discussion, I was surprised to find myself agreeing with Royar's point of view. Alice was right, there's more to life than putting yourself first. So much opens up when you question lizard-brained, survivalist thinking. But Royar wasn't contradicting Alice for the sake of it. He seemed to be talking about where good deeds come from. For once, Royar wasn't sounding selfish.

I think Alice understood this but she was taking a stronger stance with her reply.

"I'm still not sure you get it Roy. How many examples do you need before you understand we're only here because someone else, a lot of people in fact, made all kinds of sacrifices for us along the way."

Alice gave Royar a patronising smile.

"I love powerful people Royar. They're either humble like Elon Mensch, or they think they're invincible. Which are you?"

I actually felt sorry for Royar. It wasn't because Alice was being too hard on him, he had deserved much worse than this before now. Maybe I was sympathetic because Royar was being tried for past crimes. At least that's how it seemed to me.

Before Royar answered, I decided it was a good time for me to step in and shift the conversation onto something more positive.

"You're both making excellent points."

I started as inoffensively as I could, looking between Alice and Royar to keep their attention.

"Take grounding for instance. Can we really say being grounded is better for any individual? Are grounded people better for society as a whole? There's no definitive answer."

I turned to Royar as I said this because I wanted to respond to him directly. I wanted to hold Royar's focus within the group.

"Roy, your comment about Kevin and me helping ourselves was almost a vote of confidence for JT. At least until you added your final element of doubt."

Royar looked pleased his earlier jab had registered with me.

"Yes Yar, thanks for keeping our feet on the ground," Kevin said, adding his own ironic tribute.

I hoped Kevin's sarcasm didn't put Royar back on guard.

"I think you know how I feel about being here Steve. Most of the time I'd rather be somewhere else," Royar said.

There was plenty of evidence to support this up to now.

"I got that message Roy but I'm also seeing you contribute more in each session. Tonight for example, you've really been present and engaged," I said.

I hoped Royar would make the same connection. He processed this for a second before replying.

"The point you're missing Steve is zip-travel was working for me. Unlike you, I didn't give up by choice. The shutdown is clearly working for you, and for Kevin."

Royar now addressed to the circle as a whole.

"Steve quit before the shutdown so I guess he got what he wanted."

Royar looked back towards me.

"You've carved out a nice groove for yourself in this brave new world. I genuinely admire what you've done but the rest of us won't be so lucky."

I was hearing the usual contempt but for the first time there was uncertainty in Royar's voice.

"You and Kevin don't know how lucky you are," Royar said.

He threw his hands up in frustration and sat back in his chair. The room was quiet for a moment.

"If we're being honest Yar, I don't feel all that lucky," Kevin said, his voice was lower than usual.

"I didn't feel lucky when Saira died last year. I didn't feel all that lucky watching her body waste away. I don't feel lucky having to live with all these memories," Kevin tapped his temple as he spoke. "Reliving them again and again in every Journey Time session with people like you."

The harshness of Kevin's tone surprised everyone, although it was gone from his next sentence.

"I also don't feel lucky helping other people get grounded, when I'm not even sure I'm grounded myself."

Kevin's uncertainty shook me to the core. I'd relied on him so much over the years. It never occurred to me he was still grieving. Like Elon,

I'd seen Kevin as a rock but he was only human. It had taken all this time for Kevin to share the grief he was carrying, and all this time for me to see another one of my mistakes. I was about to say something to Kevin when Mila replied before me.

"Was Saira your wife?"

Mila spoke softly to Kevin, visibly shrinking from the answer.

"Yes," Kevin said. "We got married after she was diagnosed. We always planned to marry..."

Kevin's voice broke up.

"You know what it's like when you're together."

There was silence again.

Partly to dislocate myself from the guilt, but mostly because I can't stop myself, my mind was already racing away from the conversation in the room. I imagined millions of neural pathways lighting up inside all of our heads. I thought of everything each one of us could say in response to this situation, all the word combinations currently being processed and matched to emotions. I realised all this was happening in millionths of seconds as we all searched for the right thing to say.

It only took another second for seven sets of thoughts to coalesce around one voice once again.

"I lost my Dad to RC three years ago." Oran broke the silence, looking at Kevin as he spoke.

"I hated him for dying."

Oran wasn't talking to anyone in particular. This was sharing in its rawest form.

"And hating him made me hate myself," Oran finished.

"I blame myself all the time," Kevin said, taking over again. "I should have done something. Maybe stopped Saira zipping when the fvc rumours started. Do you know they can now trace RC to the exact hop? I still haven't done this. I don't think I could ever stand to know."

RC is cruel to the people it leaves behind in a way most diseases aren't. Being able to see exactly what caused a loved one's death has led to people taking their own lives. Unable to live with the guilt or the knowledge most RC deaths could have been prevented.

"I can't face knowing either," Oran said, "Any journey would be utterly pointless if it was the cause."

Oran was now staring at the floor.

"The worst thing would be finding out it was a hop we planned together," Kevin said. "A hundred years ago they called it survivor guilt. People blamed themselves for everything back then. No wonder the world was in such a mess."

The room went quiet again.

"I'm sorry Kevin, Oran," Mila said, breaking the silence again.

"You lost someone real. I made up a story."

I felt sorry for all three of them.

"It's not your fault Mila," Kevin said, managing to give her a smile.

"It is my fault." Mila said.

She spoke quietly, allowing us further into her thoughts.

"In the first session I just saw Steve the group leader, Kevin the super-confident Vet, Royar the big-time exec, Alice the super-intelligent professional and Oran the chatterbox."

Oran was upset but still seemed to enjoy the accolade.

"I didn't say anything because I was intimidated," Mila said. "But now you've all shared, I can't believe I made this mistake. You're all so much more."

"We're all so much more Mila," I said in reply. "It's what makes us human. Sharing makes us human."

Time stood still around the circle for a moment. There was no acknowledgement, no agreement. Just a few more seconds of journey time before Royar spoke again, more gently this time.

"My Granddad loved science-fiction," Royar said, looking at Mila as he spoke.

"He had all these vintage books and comics stashed away at home. His face lit up when he read them to me."

Royar's face showed a glimpse of his Granddad's light as he talked.

"Astounding Stories he called them. He loved the bizarre worlds, I loved the way everything was chrome."

The group listened as Royar spoke, no-one seemed to know where this was going.

"Telling stories made him look so much younger. I wondered why he couldn't be like that all the time."

Royar thought about this for a moment, as if something new was coming to him.

"There was one comic book cover, I think the story was about cyborg-drones in deep-space. Each drone was linked to a human operator back on earth. I can't remember much about the story but the front cover fascinated me. It was a picture of a man and a drone, split down the middle. At the bottom of the page it said, "If one half of your brain is in space, thinking about being at home, and the other half is home, thinking about being in space… Where are YOU?"

Royar leant forward in his seat, a puzzled look crossed his face.

"The more I zipped the more I thought about this picture. After a while the man in the picture was me. I was either at home dreaming of being away, or I was away and dreaming of being at home."

Royar paused for nothing more than a second.

"I knew I was lost even then."

Royar's dislocation was complete.

I'm not sure Royar planned to share as much as he did. I think Kevin might have felt the same way after talking about Saira, although in his case there would probably be less regret. If he wasn't already, Royar would soon be aware how much he had revealed and this might make him feel vulnerable. As Elon said in the handbook, "Power over words isn't power over emotion. Ignoring this gives us the false impression we're in control."

Royar and I had one thing in common at least. We were both good at suppressing our feelings, burying them deep in the past. Over the years the impulse to let things go had grown stronger for me. I don't know if Royar felt the same way but sharing these emotions would feel like a definite change. Maybe it could even be the start of some-thing new. Whatever it was, this was definitely a significant moment in Royar's grounding, and an important moment for this group.

It had stayed quiet after Royar finished speaking.

The silence held for a few seconds more before Kevin cut in.

"So what now Yar?"

"I'm not sure," Royar admitted. "I'm sorry for your loss Kevin. Oran, I'm sorry about your Dad too."

"Thanks Royar. He was a great guy," Oran said. "He was so great to me. We spent a lot of time together. Just doing normal stuff around the house and in the garden. It bored me sometimes but now they're the times I think about most. Like your Granddad's stories."

Oran and Royar thought together.

"That bike ride was the most time I spent with my Dad," Royar said. "He tried to teach me a lesson about wasting time. All it did was show me how precious our journey was."

Royar smiled to himself and shook his head, the irony wasn't lost on him.

"He loved you Roy," Oran replied to Royar unexpectedly. "Your Dad. No matter what you think about how much time he spent with you, he loved you. That's what I think anyway."

"Thank you Oran, I think I know that now too," Royar said.

I checked the clock on my quad, we'd gone almost thirty minutes past our usual finishing time. I silently thanked JT's policy of always being the last booking in any communal space. Our groups were always the last to use this hall. Today reminded me why this was so important.

· · ·

Kevin and I had been standing in the road talking for some time, mostly about Saira. We'd talked about Saira before but tonight was different because Kevin had a lot more to say.

"It's been fifty years since anyone died of cancer. Most of us forgot what it was like to watch someone waste away. She just became less and less each day."

I listened closely as Kevin spoke. There's so much to say about death and loss, but who do we say it to? The response we seem to get from everyone is 'move on'. Maybe not in so many words but no-one wants to see people they love struggling with grief.

We stood together as Kevin talked. My body felt awkward. I never knew what to do with it at times like this. Should I be stoic or give him a hug.

Kevin snapped me away from my thoughts.

"Do you remember the old alms houses at the top of the road?" he asked. "The older people who lived there would come and go."

Kevin was talking expansively now.

"At first they'd be out in all weathers, weeding, sweeping leaves, planting flowers, pruning bushes. The first sign was these little acts of care drying up. One by one each tenant lost the fight with nature when kneeling or walking became too much. Then the weeds rammed home their advantage without mercy. Then the ambulance would be there all the time. A month or so later a new resident moved in."

Kevin looked up at the sky, pushing out his jaw as he suppressed a faint tremble.

"That's what happened to Saira. She kept going but she could do less and less. In the last month she couldn't even get out of bed. I hate remembering her that way. She'd hate me for it too."

"She wouldn't," I said with real conviction, "Saira loved you. You're not remembering her right. She'd hate you for that."

It was one of the few times I knew I was absolutely right.

Kevin smiled.

"Next you'll be saying she'd want me to move on."

He studied me closely.

"No one knew Saira better than you Kev, I think you know exactly what she'd say."

We both paused to think.

"Right now she'd probably say something like, 'Are you two idiots still talking in the middle of the road?'"

Kevin's laugh was big and immediate.

"She would have said that. Thanks for the reminder Steve," Kevin said, pushing me in the direction of home.

He sounded better, although I knew it was impossible to tell.

7

"A journey is what it takes
to get somewhere worth going."
Elon Mensch

7.57pm
Wednesday 13 February 2104
Session 6

OUR LAST SESSION was emotional. Every participant had engaged, some more than others but they'd all played their part. I'd learned from experience and from the handbook that sessions like this can create hangovers. For instance, in subsequent meetings there can be a reluctance to explore any more matters of the heart.

I had no way of knowing how people would feel when we got back together. Would Royar be embarrassed after showing what he might call weakness? Would he pretend it never happened? Would he turn up at all? I asked myself the same questions about Oran, even though there was no way to be sure in either case.

I'd made a point of speaking to Kevin in the week. It had been a tough session for him but he sounded fine, good in fact. I reminded myself this was the only real evidence I had to work with. Everything else over the last two weeks was just guesswork on my part.

I thought back to the most personal points of the sharing. Kevin, Royar and Oran had all offered up something profound, not to mention new to our group. Mila and Alice had also played an integral role. Not just on the night, but also by showing the rest of us how it should be done in earlier sessions.

There was so much progress here, I was annoyed with myself for not seeing it sooner. The way people trusted each other with their deepest thoughts and feelings. There was no better measure of how far we have come.

Relationships and individual roles were changing and growing. There has been significant movement, which is everything in the grounding of this group. The huge impact of Elon's call brought us closer together. With effortless ease, Elon blew away so many unhelpful ideas of power, hierarchy and control. Along with any delusions of grandeur any of us might have, including me.

I still find it hard to believe Elon joined our session. Elena messaged me a few days afterwards. She'd heard the news about our group on the JT grapevine. After calling me all the names under the sun, Elena had a lot to say.

"I can't believe your luck. Do you know how long I've worked here? Do you know how many great coachees I've had? Just how badly did you screw up?"

I didn't try to defend myself, nor did I try to make Elena feel better.

• • •

I thought about Elon's stories again as I walked to the hall, and as I got things ready for the new session to start. The new session was slow off the mark. There was a noticeable buzz at the very beginning. People were pleased to see each other and looked like they wanted to talk, but after that the conversation stalled.

I imagined people might have questions about where all this was going. Grounding could be frustrating like that. You feel as if you're getting somewhere but there's not much to hold on to. I remember Elon being challenged about this years ago. His response was, "Life doesn't come with a handrail."

Back in the circle, at least the exchanges weren't dying out completely. Mila shared some thoughts from her recent journaling. Alice told us how she felt about her sharing so far. I was glad to hear Alice say on the whole she felt good. Oran never let any silence last too long but there were none of the 10,000 volt moments we'd come to expect. I started to worry whether this group might have been spoiled. How Elon's appearance might be too big for anything else to live up to. Even Kevin seemed quieter than usual tonight.

The talking managed to make its way once around the circle but it was far from flowing. Kevin and I played our standard defibrillation card by suggesting a break. We both hoped the physical movement would get things going, or at least change the mood.

There wasn't much difference when we came back for the second half. The group couldn't seem to get away from the small talk. The longer this went on, the more anxious I became. I told myself not to worry and that everything would be okay. For the time being at least, the small talk was making people feel safe.

Whenever sharing moves slowly, vets and group leaders are there to stop it grinding to a halt. We were definitely getting close to another intervention point. I scoured the handbook in my mind to think of an appropriate mid-programme exercise. Kevin and I had discussed a few options at moments like this in the past. We could always take the lead with new stories, although both of us think more sharing from us risks stemming the participant's flow altogether.

I thought back to my training and my previous session work. I remember something I wrote in my e-copy of the handbook.

"Wherever possible, let your group talk. A new direction (for sharing) is always possible as long as they're talking."

I can't remember who said this to me or whether it was a direct quote. It didn't matter, the sentiment sounded right. It reminded me the small talk always leads somewhere. In my experience this was true, although right now I was expecting my faith in this to be proved wrong.

Royar and Alice were now talking about diamond commodities. The subject had been a recent news story after the forevermark had been successfully faked once again. As they talked I remembered a friend of mine who was an artist. I found it incredible when he told me about his respect for professional counterfeiters. I asked him how someone who creates art could have any time for people who use their talent to steal. He said the fakers are talented in their own right and besides, "Anyone who makes a living selling their own art gets my respect."

I realised this story was just another distraction.

• • •

Back in the conversation, Alice was now talking about her visit to a diamond mine in Botswana. She talked about a village she went to on the same trip. Although it wasn't far away, the village had no zjt pods, so it was a five-hour jeep ride from where she was staying. Alice looked like she was enjoying re-living this story. Mila found it more interesting as the conversation moved away from diamonds and shifted instead into the sights, sounds and smells of the Tuli Bock countryside.

As Alice came to a natural pause Mila got more involved.

Slightly embarrassed at first, Mila talked about her imaginary trips to Jodphur and Rajasthan. How they had such an impact on her as she devoured all of the history and photos she could find. She said one day she wanted to visit the places from her stories, so she could compare the reality with her ideas. Mila would have happily said more, but this time it was Oran doing the interrupting.

"I've zipped to India and Sri Lanka a lot," he began. "I managed to get off the beaten track a few times too."

For the first time tonight, Oran's tone sounded like the beginning of something more than just small talk.

"I remember being just outside Colombo. I'd zipped there on a whim after a friend told me how amazing it was. I'd been to Sri Lanka but never out in the sticks, so I had no idea what to expect. My zip-in went fine but there was a power-cut in the village which meant I couldn't zip out."

Oran's shoulders rose and fell as he sighed. Something about this memory made him feel insecure, but he'd made up his mind up to go on.

"There was only one pod. The family who owned it were great. I don't think I've ever had so much tea and sympathy while I was stuck there. They were really kind, and I must have seemed so odd."

I wondered if this was why Oran looked so uncomfortable as he shared this experience.

"I tried to hide how keen I was to zip out but I'd already started sweating. That was when I knew I was having a full on panic attack."

Oran swallowed hard, his interlocked fingers pressed tightly together in his lap.

"My heart was pounding. I imagined the blood rushing back and forth in my chest. I thought to myself, 'This is it, I'm going to die here'. Any minute now I'll have a heart attack or one of my arteries will just tear itself apart with the strain."

Oran pressed his chest, breathing heavily as he spoke.

"This is what happens. I get to a point where I can't deal with the fear, so I give in to the panic. I was almost at the point of giving in, when this little kid brought over a picture book and dropped it in my lap."

Oran smiled, remembering this kid broke his anxiety all over again.

"She was so little, maybe not even three. I didn't see her at first. I just felt the book as she dropped it on my lap."

He shook his head in disbelief.

"I watched as she climbed onto the chair next to me, without saying a word. My chest was still heaving, it seemed to take ages but she wouldn't give up. Then when she was set on the chair, this little thing just looked at me and pointed to the book."

Oran had tensed up when he talked about his panic attack but the tension in his body had now disappeared.

The whole scene was so clear in my mind. Oran panicking, desperately trying to hold himself together, and just as he was losing the fight, this child intervened. Of course I didn't know what any of it really looked like. The house, the family, the village but it didn't matter. The colours were vibrant in my mind. The house and the people were caring and warm. The child herself was a bundle of positive energy. Whether she had seen Oran panicking or not, she had willed herself onto that chair. Applying every fibre of her body to this single task, the way toddlers do.

I realise I'm getting carried away with Oran's story.

"Let him paint the pictures," I think to myself, "It's his story after all."

I also notice Royar studying me as I'm thinking. I hope the look on my face conveyed concentrated interest alone.

"So this little kid ended my panic attack," Oran continued. "The only non-medical thing that ever did."

Oran smiled again to himself.

"I spent the next half-hour reading a story about a dog who could drive a car, go shopping and play tennis. Slowly my body came back to normal. My chest stopped heaving, then the power came back on. I thanked the family, gave the little girl a hug and zipped-out. I can't remember the rest of their names, but I think her name was Sachini?"

Remembering the child's name pleased Oran. He wasn't sure if it was right but the feeling behind the memory was one of pure thanks. Sharing this story was a good grounding moment for him.

"The same thing happened to me but I was at my in-laws in Michigan," Kevin said.

Everyone around the circle laughed at this.

"It happened to me too," Alice said.

I thought to myself how good it was to see this session finally come to life.

"I went to Costa Rica and my quad lost the grid. I was there with a friend but that didn't stop me freaking out. I think it was seeing the red light and the screen saying 'Searching…'. And the emergency tone, I'd never heard that tone before."

Alice was getting into her story the same way Oran did.

"The exact same thing happened," Alice said, focusing on Oran. "My heart started racing, I felt the sheerest panic I've ever known."

Alice imitated her rising sense of panic.

"What have I done? Why did I come here? Is this where I'm going to die? My friend realised I was panicking but the moment she began comforting me, the signal returned and we were back on the grid."

Alice finished with a warm smile for Oran.

"My friends laughed at me for ages about this. Some of them still do."

It went quiet for a moment.

"I feel stupid now," Oran said, his tone was reflective. "I mean, zjt has been offline for two years but back then I freaked out after less than an hour."

"At least it wasn't less than a minute," Alice laughed but Oran remained serious.

"It makes me wonder if I ever really travelled," Oran said, wrestling with this question now.

"Like Elon said, and Steve said it at the beginning, I visited all these places but did I ever let go? Somewhere or something else was always with me. No one place was ever good enough."

Oran took a deep breath.

"I don't want to be like that any more," he spoke clearly. "I want to be present where I am now."

I wanted this too.

Oran was right, I never really travelled when I was zipping. This struck me again the moment Oran talked about being present. In the past I went to different places but there was no real relationship for me there. Getting there and coming back only took seconds so how could I expect to adjust.

Oran carried on piecing things together. He started writing notes in his journal. I used the brief lull to thank Alice and Oran for sharing again. I re-affirmed that it was a good thing everyone was now sharing and recalling stories this way. My recap was probably unnecessary but I explained grounding wasn't just taking trips down memory lane. The entire process is about discovering who we are and where we want to be.

I continued my explanation.

"Oran and Alice gave us another good example of what grounding feels like. Stitching together important lessons from our experiences, even the unpleasant ones. The more we share, the more we learn. The more we learn, the better we understand our lives today."

I paused for a moment to think about what I wanted to say.

"And don't worry if you haven't felt anything yet," I said.

Royar looked up from his quad.

"It doesn't matter how many times you hear or see someone else grounding. You only feel the real impact when it happens to you."

This sounded preachy but it was too late to think about that now.

"There ends the sermon from Pastor Steve," I thought to myself, hoping the group would focus on the message and ignore the delivery.

We still had about ten minutes to go but it felt like a good time to wrap things up. Kevin sensed this too and asked if there was anything else people wanted to talk about or revisit. As Kevin did this I motioned to Oran that he could talk to us after the session if he wanted. Rightly or wrongly I sensed there was something he might want to say without an audience. Oran and I did grab a few seconds as the group broke up but he seemed happy enough. He had no burning desire to talk about anything, although he said he would like more time to think.

I assured Oran this was the right response. He clutched his journal and his quad tightly to his chest as we spoke. I thought about how intimate our relationships with these devices has become. How that intimacy goes even further when we used quads to record our closest thoughts.

As Oran and I talked, Alice and Kevin finished the usual chores. I noticed there was a lot more laughter than stacking chairs usually creates. Oran watched the two of them together. I tried to guess what he was thinking.

He turned back to me and started putting on his coat.

"Are Kevin and Agnieszka a couple now?" Oran asked.

I decided not to answer his question, it could have been rhetorical anyway. The subject of Alice and Kevin's relationship felt like the wrong conversation to be having with Oran. In any case Oran was happy enough not to push for an answer. Instead he said goodnight and headed for the door.

• • •

Kevin was quiet on our walk home. I wondered if it had anything to do with not seeing Alice for another two weeks. Kevin was now checking his quad as we walked, something I'd never know him to do.

"Important message?" I asked as he tapped out what looked like a quick reply on his screen.

"Not really. Just setting myself a reminder to get more meds before we next meet. You wouldn't believe the concoction of mood-suppressants I have to take before I listen to you."

Kevin looked at me with a wink, I answered in kind.

"I don't do meds any more. I stick to long runs, casual stalking and going through recycling. It's amazing what people throw away."

In reality I do none of these things, although I can imagine some people might find it easy to think that I do. I admit to being somewhat fascinated by people with this level of obsession. I wonder about their experiences and their lives. What drives them and what tips them over the edge.

"You know I'll never feel safe again after hearing you say that," Kevin said in reply.

We reached the top of my road, Kevin waved and walked away up the hill. He was already back on his quad. At a guess I'd say he was messaging Alice and she was messaging him back. I couldn't know any of this for sure but our last chat about Saira was making more sense. So was Kevin's sharing in the previous session. His feelings were definitely changing, or re-emerging.

As I walked home, I decided that in my perfect world neither Alice nor Kevin deserved to be alone, especially if they wanted to be together. I wondered to myself what it must feel like. To meet someone you want to share so much with, despite all the uncertainty.

I thought about all of the vulnerability that comes with this level of union. The pain of loss when someone close leaves you or dies. I know how much Kevin loved Saira and how much he missed their togetherness after she was gone. Perhaps moving on and finding a new closeness with Alice was the only way to honour his previous relationship. I convinced myself Saira would want this for Kevin. Then I tried to imagine what Saira would want for me but nothing came to mind.

For some bizarre reason I tried to imagine what my life would have been like with Saira or Alice. Nothing came to mind.

There was a blank, then there was Mila, then the thoughts and pictures immediately began to cascade.

I imagined a relationship that could be the ultimate expression of sharing. A true and unflinching sharing of lives, and everything this means. Nothing hidden. A mutual knowledge deeper than any veneer. All the warts, anxieties, dislocations and depressions shared openly.

The force of my emotions surprised me.

"I wonder if this is something I could talk to Kevin about," I asked myself.

I have no idea why this was the first question in my mind.

"Because you'll never talk about it with Mila," was my answering thought as I arrived home.

8

"Don't be scared of the odd argument.
A good scrap always comes before a good spell of peace."
Elon Mensch

7.12pm
Wednesday 27 February 2104
Session 7

OVER THE LAST few days I've thought a lot about Oran. I've wondered how much time he really gave himself since our last session. I could rely on Mila to think carefully but I wasn't so sure in Oran's case. Of all the participants, Oran seemed to be having the hardest time adjusting to his post-shutdown life. This was my conclusion after last time anyway.

Oran has done more than his fair share of the talking but there's a difference between talking and sharing. I remind myself Oran shared with Kevin last time round. What he said about his Dad was real enough.

Oran was the person who had talked the most and here I was deciding he might have said the least.

"Way to work with the evidence Steve," I thought to myself.

Kevin's nickname for Oran was 'Grout', because he was, 'made to filling gaps'. As well as working on major engineering projects Kevin did a lot of work around the home. Grout was a good name for Oran but it probably had more to do with Kevin recently re-decorating his bathroom. In my experience, only Kevin could turn home improvement into philosophy.

I thought some more about Oran's willingness to talk. He was a gap filler but I think this is because he wants to be in the middle of everything. Being a focus point, maybe even a source of entertainment for the other people in the group was what Oran seemed to enjoy more than anything else.

As I carried on walking it felt like my thoughts about Oran were going somewhere.

"It's true Oran likes to entertain but does he do it to please himself or other people?" I wondered, reaching the outer doors of the hall.

Is trying to please people a distraction for Oran? What is it distracting him from? Perhaps Oran's grounding journey is about creating gaps for himself. More times when he can step back and let others do the talking, perhaps allowing him to focus on what's going on inside. Maybe learning to listen rather than just waiting for the next opportunity to speak?

"Maybe Oran will learn to love silence one day?"

I laughed to myself at this thought. It was possible of course but it didn't seem likely today.

• • •

The new session started well. Everyone was engaging in a discussion about the shutdown, particularly their adjustment experiences over the last few years.

"I'm not sure I'd survive in a hard-travel world. Everyone I know, everything I enjoy doing relied on zjt. My life just doesn't work without it."

Oran was still happy to fill any silences right now.

"You and everyone else," Royar replied, his voice somewhat gentler than his words. "For the last two years we've all been in the same boat."

"Good of you to notice Royar," Oran said in return, "But I don't think you get it. Everyone I know lives somewhere else. Yes I can move but I need to figure our where to go first. I'm not spending 22 hours on a plane just to fly back here six months later."

Maybe this was the big sticking point for Oran. The JT handbook describes how some people think about all forms of travel in zip-travel terms. This means a short-haul flight or even a walk to the local shops can seem like a huge overhead. In zjt terms this would be years of journey time all coming at once. The whole idea of dragging your body from one place to another could feel like an eternal struggle. Oran was feeling stuck in one place and his only option was to hard-travel out. But the hard-travel option was something he was denying himself.

Kevin picked up the topic while I stayed with my thoughts.

"Our Grandparents were the last generation to hard-travel everywhere. They really put in the hours. Some of them even flew thousands of miles every month."

The thought of this was incredible to everyone. No one knew journey time like our predecessors.

Kevin carried on in the same vein.

"I'm the same as you Oran, but hard-travel isn't the big deal we make it. Staying here or going somewhere else doesn't have to feel like a life sentence. If you go somewhere else and decide you don't like it, you can always come back."

Kevin had made a good point. Maybe Oran could see his situation in a way that didn't make him feel stuck.

"It's sweet of you Kevin but you're wide of the mark. I haven't hard travelled since Canada because I don't know where to go."

Oran was doing his best to keep it under wraps but his frustration was rising.

"That makes sense Oran. Sorry if I didn't acknowledge this before now. If Saira was here she'd have put me right for sure," Kevin said.

Mentioning Saira came a lot easier to him this time.

"I like the sound of Saira more and more," said Mila, laughing at the idea of someone keeping Kevin in check.

"Maybe we can straighten Kevin out together?" Alice said to Mila with a big smile on her face.

"I'd like to see that Alice," Kevin replied. "You should know I've had plenty of practice learning how to duck."

Kevin looked back towards Oran. I thought it might help if I picked up the same thread.

"Joking aside Oran, this could be the right time for a deeper exploration of your choices," I said, trying to give him another angle on the same suggestion.

"You might feel stuck right now but you still have a choice. Stay here, go somewhere else, base yourself in a couple of places, change your mind if you want to. I know hard-travel's a bigger choice than zipping used to be but it's not a one way ticket or a one shot deal."

I did my best to make sure this was conventional JT exposition.

Although he was quiet, Royar appeared to be following the conversation. There had been some tell tale signs he was listening but now he appeared to reach some kind of conclusion.

"Nice try chaps," Royar said looking at Kevin and me. "You can lead a horse to water but you can't make it drink."

This was Royar's final thought on the discussion so far. It occurred to me that sympathy for Royar had grown after he shared in the last session. If that sympathy was a flickering flame, the look on one or two of the faces around the circle suggested he had just blown it out.

Mila was the first to confirm this pet theory.

"I'm sorry Roy, what did you just say?" Mila challenged him openly.

"Take it easy Mila," Royar said, holding a hand up in apology.

Royar was sensitive enough to detect something he said had annoyed her.

"All I meant was, if Oran can't decide no one can make him. What I actually said was, you can lead a horse to water but you can't make it drink. I'm sorry if you found that offensive." Royar's apology sounded sincere.

Something had offended Mila, she had rounded on him but Royar hadn't replied with an attack. I noted how much of a change this was from the Royar we'd all experienced in the first half of the programme.

"I thought that's what you said," Mila said, ignoring Royar's apology. "I hate that phrase, it's a cop out. What you're saying about Oran is deeply offensive."

Kevin looked at me and then over to Alice, he looked delighted someone else was taking Royar to task. Royar no longer sounded genuine but he remained calm with his reply.

"I'm sorry Mila, I didn't mean to offend you or Oran, but this is a storm in a tea cup, let's not turn it into an issue. All Oran has to do is own his situation. None of us can choose for him. As Kevin said, we're all battling the same thing."

Royar paused, trying to adopt an even more conciliatory tone.

"If you don't like what you're hearing, don't shoot the messenger," he said.

I wasn't about to get involved but I didn't appreciate Royar's last turn of phrase either. Some messengers get a kick out of delivering bad news, and they deserve to be held accountable when they do.

Royar was undoing himself with clichés.

Mila listened to what Royar had to say but a raw nerve had been touched and she wasn't finished returning the pain.

"The thing is Roy, I don't like what I'm hearing and I can't let it go. Narrow-minded stuff like that bullshit horse saying is used to keep people down. To keep people in their place and make sure they stay there."

Mila's feelings were strong on this subject and she was making them clear.

"You're saying Oran is being stubborn, the way a horse is stubborn when it refuses to jump a fence or take a drink. That's the message I don't like, and it's completely the messenger's fault. You're also trying to absolve yourself from any part in what Oran's going through. And you're piling even more pressure on him for refusing to see an obvious way out, and not accepting our support."

Before today Mila might never have found the courage to take Royar to task. Maybe it was Alice's example she was following. Maybe it was something Elon said. Maybe she felt bolder after getting some of her own insecurities out of the way. Maybe she was just sticking up for a friend. Whatever the reason, Mila was showing a new found confidence.

Royar had listening closely to Mila's criticism. This was exactly the kind of cut and thrust conflict he relished. The more Mila became personally involved the more interesting this was to Royar. I thought about my first argument with Royar but he was in a different place now.

In any event Mila wasn't finished.

"No one refuses anything if they think it will help them. What you're calling a refusal might be Oran protecting himself or wanting to think more deeply about his situation. Maybe he's battling something else, you don't know. Oran's human, he's not a horse. A horse may have a thousand reasons not to drink the water you lead him to but that has nothing to do with thinking and reason."

"Keep going Mila, I think you're on to something," Royar said.

He was still calm but Royar wasn't used to waiting this long. This was a deliberate poke to make Mila lose her temper and appear out of control.

"I don't need your permission to keep going Roy and I will carry on."

Mila's tone was still angry but it was also even.

"If Oran or anyone else isn't ready to make a choice, who are you to judge. It's up to him whether he accepts your assistance or your opinion. Kevin, you might also want to take note."

Up to now Mila's frustration with Royar seemed to have the support of the room. Turning on Kevin would only serve split that support.

Mila turned to Oran who by now was looking uncomfortable.

"I'm sorry Oran, I didn't mean to talk about you like you weren't there. Not everyone in this room thinks like Royar. I want you to know, you have my total respect and admiration for being honest about where you are."

Mila's voice was stressed but sincere.

"Not many of us have the same courage when we're in that place. I also think you're absolutely right to be stuck with your choice."

Mila expanded her argument further, looking back to Royar as she did.

"I think we all know when someone genuinely wants to engage with us or when they're just going through the motions. We can all tell when the person in front of us is listening or not. Whether they have a real interest to connect with us or talk down to us."

Mila looked towards Kevin and me as she said this. Perhaps this was the point she wanted to make to him, perhaps she was separating Kevin and I from Royar. Right now it was hard for me to tell.

The temperature of Mila's speech was finally descending. She started speaking slowly, more deliberately as her point drew closer to an end.

"I don't need anyone else to agree with me, but I want you all to know where I'm coming from. We're all people here and we deserve to be treated like people. And like equals."

She sat back in her chair. I thought she might shy away from Royar's right to reply, maybe by leaving the room or not letting him speak. In the end it didn't matter because Royar's reply was by no means an attack or even a warring defence. Something Mila said must have changed Royar's mind. Either that or he decided for his own reasons that his usual response no longer felt right. Instead he spoke softly, looking directly at everyone he named.

"Mila, I'm sorry if I offended you, I really am. Oran, Mila's right, that was the wrong thing for me to say. It was dismissive and I made you sound foolish for being stuck on a difficult question. All I can do is apologise," he said.

Royar sounded genuinely sincere.

I thought about the JT handbook as Royar spoke, specifically the section on group leadership that talks about allowing disagreements to play themselves out. 'Peer-defence' Elon calls it in the book. It means that if someone is willing to step into a discussion on behalf of another member of the group, this is positive for the circle. We'd already seen it in this group with Alice and Royar, although Royar's response was completely different this time around.

I was careful not to let my thoughts drift too far. A few seconds had already passed in silence, perhaps the ideal point for me to say something had passed. Maybe I should have picked up on Oran's dilemma and more actively supported him as he tried to address it. Mila wasn't completely right in her argument, we could all be more equine than human in our thinking at times.

There was no point blaming myself for missing the opportunity to say or do something earlier, no one can turn back time. I decided instead that right now was the best time to enter the debate.

"I think we're getting closer to the reason, or reasons why we're all here. At least that's how it feels to me."

As usual I started in bland terms.

"I also think there's a lot of alignment in the way we're thinking about our choices. At no point did I hear anyone say this wasn't Oran's decision to make. All I heard was a difference of opinion and some tension because we all know his decision isn't be easy."

I knew these were thinly veiled attempts at reconciliation. I also knew this was taking fence-sitting to Olympic heights but this was also how I felt. Not just about Oran but about grounding for everyone.

"Mila, we all need to feel equally supported, I think you made that point passionately. It's up to all of us not to let that principle go.

Not to hold ourselves back if we feel stuck, unsupported, misunderstood or mistreated. Grounding is about dealing with reality. Our reality. Our lives in fewer places, whether those places are here, somewhere else or any other combination."

I noticed Oran looking unsettled again so I asked him directly.

"Oran, is there something you wanted to say?"

There was quiet as Oran thought, then spoke.

"I guess I never expected to be this static for this long. I just miss all the other people and places so much."

Oran's voice trailed off.

It was clear now wasn't the right time for Oran to make any kind of decision but I was convinced tonight would be an important step in the right direction for him. Oran could give himself permission to think about this question and not feel stupid, frustrated or stubborn for needing more time. Maybe this would lead to him feeling less stuck.

It didn't feel like there was much more to be said in this session. After wrapping things up, I watched Royar walk over to Mila. He had his back to me but I could see she was smiling. His gestures looked apologetic, friendly even. I hoped these were all signals the quarrel wasn't something either of them had plans to carry on.

• • •

Kevin and I walked home under an empty sky.

When I was younger I went through a phase of studying all of the different kinds of helicopters, planes, balloons and everything else that used to fill the sky a hundred years ago.

We had planes today, more so in the last year, but it was still quite rare to see one. I carried on looking up, imagining con-trails dissecting the sky. I thought about all the excited people on jet-liners travelling to far-away places when they were still thought of as far-away.

More thoughts careered through my mind as I stared. I wondered how many different types of planes there actually were. I knew about business jets, fighters and huge transporters carrying people and machinery all over the world but I also knew there must have been more.

"Missing something?" Kevin said, as he watched me staring upwards into space.

"I usually am," was my wiseacre reply.

"It's always the same when you go quiet. You're the only person I know who continually gets lost on a ten minute walk home."

I laugh in response to this.

"My Mum used to say one day I'd walk under a bus. Then I'd remind her all the buses were in museums. She'd say it was a turn of phrase and give me one of Saira's famous clips around the ear."

I mimed rubbing my ear to make the point.

"A turn of phrase like horses to water? Those old sayings will get you in trouble Steve."

Kevin spoke in a mock-scolding voice, neatly reviving the subject of the night.

"Mila is almost unrecognisable from the first session," I said in reply.

"But I also have to admit to liking Royar more and more. He was the bigger person tonight. If that was the first session he would never have given way."

I finished talking as we reached the top of my road.

"Careful Steve, you'll be inviting certain participants over to dinner next," Kevin said.

"Like the first programme, I know."

This was an error of judgement I'd rather forget.

Kevin walked away up the hill snorting in amusement.

I walked home thinking about the last time I had anyone over to the house.

9

"Life throws a lot your way,
think of grounding as extra catching practice."
Elon Mensch

7.42pm
Wednesday 12 March 2104
Session 8

THERE WAS A real buzz in the room as this new session got underway. Everyone had heard the news. Oran was last to arrive, looking flushed he delivered it again, gasping for air between his words.

"The new <u>firmware</u> is out!"

This was the most excited anyone had been.

Alice looked towards Kevin, then turned in my direction. I deliberately avoided her eyes, not wanting to steal Oran's thunder by diverting any attention.

"There are no bugs in it this time, it's 100% clean. <u>Greyhound</u> have just announced all continental terminals will be back up next week. Most private grids have been online since the East Coast woke up yesterday morning. Zip traffic is already up to 50% of peak-prime. I knew this would happen. Steve, I told you the shutdown wouldn't last."

There was no triumph, no superiority and no malice in Oran's voice, all I could hear was joy. Oran was a kid again and it was Christmas. The missing pieces of his life were coming back to him all in one go. His family in France, his friends in St Petersburg, his old workplaces in Atlanta, Goiania and London. All of these people and places would soon be there again and he couldn't wait.

"Steve, I know we've got a couple of sessions left and I want to come. I wanted to say to everyone, it's my intention to see this through. Besides, it'll be even easier now. Wherever I am I'll just zip-in."

Oran looked and sounded sincere, although it was hard to imagine him keeping his promise.

Kevin laughed, "Zipping to your last few grounding sessions. Can we allow that Steve?"

He already knew the answer. This was just another one of Kevin's great setup lines.

"You know we can allow it Kevin."

I answered for the benefit of the room before turning back to Oran.

"Get here however you can Oran. You wouldn't be the first to zip to a grounding session. I know plenty of people who did this before the shutdown. We all want you to be here, whatever else is going on in your life, okay?"

I didn't usually like to speak for the group but in this case it felt fine.

We'd all considered the impact of this news already but Oran helped us think about it all over again.

This was another massive event in all of our lives, and it would change everything all over again.

•   •   •

Before Oran arrived we'd already been talking about the switch-on. Details were still sketchy but the consensus was it was happening and within a matter of weeks the grid would be back up worldwide.

I hadn't been able to stop thinking of all the new possibilities. My mind was already racing away. Elena had called my thinking style "peripatetic" in her final summary of my suitability for JT leadership.

"Steve can't help but follow a train of thought," Elena had said, "and his mind is like Grand Central Station."

After looking up 'peripatetic' in the dictionary, I agreed with everything she said.

Coming back to the news, days like today were seismic. We'd now had two days like this in our lifetime. I remembered part of a speech Elon made about two years ago on the day of the shutdown.

"Imagine a big switch," he said. "Picture one of those giant switches you see in the movies. A big industrial switch you need both hands to pull. The kind of switch that never gets pulled by accident. You have to get past a locked shield, into a locked cage, via a secure basement filled with armed guards."

Elon was a master at building mental pictures.

"If you can imagine that switch, today we set that big switch to 'Off'. But that switch isn't going anywhere. I'm pretty sure one day we'll be turning it back on."

It was a strange thing for the owner of Journey Time to say but he knew his fight wasn't with zjt. As always I believe Elon was fighting to open people's eyes.

There were times when grounding didn't matter, even at Journey Time. Sometimes I didn't even think grounding was the most important thing we did. On a night like tonight, this is what I wanted to say the group. I wanted to tell them we should all be as excited as Oran. This was huge news for us all.

I wanted to share with Oran that I was as excited as he was about the new firmware. Finally the world would make sense again and everyone who wanted to zip, could zip. I found it strange to think I was being given the choice once again. I'd thought about this often, wondering how much I'd be tempted but in this moment I felt more grounded than ever before.

Even with the new firmware and all the credits I'd saved, I knew I'd never step into another pod and travel that way again. I knew the switch-on, if that's what this really was, would re-complete so many lives, the way it would for Oran. In a different way the switch-on would re-confirm mine.

Everyone in the group was focused on Oran and the same internal questions. I broke away from my thoughts and found myself trying to sum up the feeling in the room.

"There's no doubt yesterday and today are big days. Oran has confirmed it. Today means changes for all of us. We can talk about those changes now if you want. Most of us are sure to be thinking about what to do next."

"You're right Steve," Oran added. "I want to talk about how this affects me. I want to hear what everyone else has to say too."

I confirmed to the group we were here to discuss whatever they wanted. I also confirmed that the rest of our sessions would run as scheduled, even if only one person turned up. I asked if everyone wanted to continue tonight. To my surprise they immediately said yes.

Whatever their individual feelings on this news, the renewed discussion Oran sparked had reminded us there were still plenty of questions. As we talked, the exchanges were upbeat and there were plenty of smiles all round. New questions and stories were shared. A variety of subjects went back and forth, most of them were light and funny. There was genuine joy and strong notes of relief.

Oran laughed loudly at something Mila said, he even gave Kevin a playful shove. He talked excitedly about all the places he would visit again. Oran also joked about all the lives that had been empty while he was away.

Royar was quiet but he also looked relieved. He was sat back in his chair, taking everything in. Despite Oran and Mila's excitement I had the feeling Royar would remember tonight longer than anyone else. It seemed to me that everything Royar had worked hard for would now be coming back to him. The life he'd built for himself, the security, his family, the rewards, the status and the respect. Most of this would come back to him via zjt.

During the break I asked Royar why he came back at all tonight, and why he hadn't left before now. He smiled warmly and told me to ask him the same question at the end of the session. It struck me as an unusual request, but it revealed he had something to say.

The second half of the session felt much like the first. Kevin and I asked if everyone really wanted to meet for the final session after today. The appetite to meet was still there but already it didn't feel as strong as before.

As a group we decided to keep the next session as scheduled, with the option to cancel if people changed their minds. Neither Kevin nor I had been here before but I could tell we both thought the same thing. That this was probably going to be the last time we would all meet, in this format at least.

Kevin told us he'd only seen the same enthusiasm for return meetings once before, and that was at a kamikaze pilots' reunion.

• • •

At the end of the session Royar was slow to gather his things. I thought he might have forgotten his request but as Kevin walked towards the door with Alice and the others, Royar made his way over to me.

"So what's the story Royar," I asked, "Why did you come back?"

He looked much more relaxed than usual. Really relaxed, not just in control of himself the way he always tried to be. Royar was clearly working less hard to appear calm.

"I knew this was coming Steve. A friend tipped me off about the new firmware last month."

Royar's calm was becoming a little clearer.

"I don't know why I stuck with the group after I found out. I thought at first it might have been an ego thing, then I became curious. I wanted to see how things would play out. Let's be honest, I also had time on my hands."

This sounded more like the detached Royar I knew.

"Don't get me wrong, if the news had been made public in week one or any session before tonight, you probably wouldn't have seen me again. Most of the time I only pitied everyone here. You more than anyone else."

This last comment stung a me a little but I chose not to reply. In any case Royar wasn't finished sharing.

"Tonight was different." He looked down momentarily. "At first I couldn't take my eyes off of Oran. I was happy for him. I had planned to come and say my goodbyes, then I changed my mind and decided to leave when Oran finished filling you all in."

For the first time it felt like Royar was talking to me as an equal, although I was immediately suspicious of this feeling.

"I kept looking over at you while Oran was speaking, but you wouldn't turn away, not even to Alice or Kevin. I thought this news would be the end of your world. I'll be honest, I thought you'd be crying or laughing in hysterics. I wanted to see your face. To see how you'd react when your little world fell apart. But you just sat there, listening to Oran, taking it in. Carrying on as if it was just another session."

Royar's speech wasn't making me feel good but he seemed to be going somewhere with it. I hoped it was heading somewhere other than more point-scoring and gloating.

Everyone apart from Kevin and Alice had now left. They were chatting, still sat in the circle.

"I could tell you were happy for Oran," Royar said, assuring himself I was interested in what he had to say.

"But the more you spoke to the group, the more I realised you were putting us first."

Royar sounded surprised by this.

"As you, Alice, Kevin, Mila and the others spoke, I was moved. I thought I had no more business being here but I found myself not wanting to leave. I forgot about not caring about being grounded and just enjoyed being here for a change."

This was quite the revelation for Royar. The session was over but he was still sharing.

"I'll be honest with you again Steve, I probably won't come back for the final session because I don't know what's going to happen to me when everything comes back on. I guess I'll find out soon enough."

Royar thought for a moment longer.

"Technically my contract is still live. I didn't think I'd ever say it but I actually hope this isn't the last time I'm here. In a perfect world I'd like to see what happens next. To find out where everyone goes."

Despite my previous experiences, I believed every one of Royar's words. It was difficult to take in and all much more than I expected. I'd steeled myself for another attack at the end of the session. Another told-you-so lecture that would finish with me under the heel of Royar's boot, and leave me with no doubt whose life had been torn to shreds.

There was probably more I would have said in response but a call came in and Royar took it immediately on his quad. He listened for a moment but was already backing his way towards the door. It seemed like he would be leaving after all.

Royar managed to wave an apologetic goodbye before turning and walking out of the door. I guessed the call was either from his office or his wife, most likely his office. Now I was sure none of us would see him again.

Despite all the hours of evidence and hope to the contrary, the last few minutes felt like a loss. When forced to make a choice Royar was no different after all.

No different to any one of us trying to do the right thing and make sense of our lives, past, present and future.

• • •

Alice said a lingering goodbye to Kevin and left the hall shortly after Royar. I was still thinking about what Royar had said. I thought about the other people in his life before and after the shutdown. All the people he had dismissed or looked down on. I knew how empty a life like that feels and couldn't figure out why someone would go back to it willingly.

I thought how Royar wouldn't believe he had a choice. Or how he would justify returning to his old life as a no-brainer. It was the life where he was important, where he was doing well for himself and his family after all.

I thought how the same was true for me.

I made a choice and was living the life I thought was best. I knew I was no better and no worse than Royar in that respect. For some strange reason the next thing I imagined a line of people in front and behind me. The line was made up of all the people I had met throughout my life, including the people I would meet in my future. I had absolutely no idea which of these people I had delighted and whom I had wronged. More likely I had done neither. Wrapped up in a world of my own thoughts, I decided most people wouldn't even have noticed me.

I felt a wave of regret for all the interactions and relationships I've avoided. How I lost the battle to the safety and benignity of tumbling conversations and streams of consciousness in my head. I stood at the door waiting for Kevin as he made his way over from the kitchen. As we locked the door and turned down the path, the cool night welcomed us with a few drops of rain.

"Another uneventful night at JT," Kevin said as we started walking.

"The night of the big switch on," I said looking up at the sky, "and the news I can't stop thinking about is that Royar has a heart."

"I saw you two chatting. I thought you were getting your final volley of abuse, or Yar's Revenge as I call it."

Kevin laughed in a self-satisfied way but I still didn't get the joke.

"I expected that too but that's not what I got."

We turned into the road at the end of the path.

"I should know by now that there's no point trying to second guess people. They'll always surprise you."

In my experience this was consistently true, not to mention something I continually forgot. It amazes me how little we know about other people and how willing we are to fill in the gaps.

"So what was Yar's surprise. He's not going to zip? He wants to join us at JT?"

Kevin jolted me back into our chat.

"The surprise is I think he might be grounded, or at least on his way," I said.

Everything about this statement was wrong, except my complete conviction that it was right.

"You have to be kidding. Are you feeling OK?"

Kevin pressed his hand to my forehead as we reached our splitting point in the road.

"I'm fine. Still processing but fine."

This was true. I was still collecting my thoughts as I spoke.

"Roy started out by telling me how scared he thought I would be by the big switch-on. He said he couldn't wait to see my face and see my world fall apart," I said.

"Nice," said Kevin, "I thought you said he had a heart?"

"He does. I think the sharing really got to him. The fact you and I weren't putting ourselves first. When I didn't crumble I think he realised something was missing."

"Kindness? Inner-strength? Concern for other people's welfare? He's missing a lot more too if you asked me," Kevin said, he obviously wasn't convinced Royar had changed at all.

"Today would have been the end of my world if my world was just JT," I said, trying to finish my earlier thought. "I always thought today would be a long way off. That even if a new firmware came along, people would take their time going back to zjt. Maybe I've been running from this day. I was okay with the way things were going..."

I was rambling and felt relieved when Kevin interrupted.

"I think everyone felt that way to some degree. We all tried to move on after zjt, then this happens. It's like going back for more after being dumped. There'll always be a nagging doubt it will happen again," Kevin said.

I thought Kevin was absolutely right about this.

"It's exactly like that," I said, excited that Kevin expressed my feelings so perfectly. "I never trusted myself completely, until today. Then it came to me during the session, I knew I'd never go back. That's why today didn't freak me out."

Finally I had expressed my feelings in a way that made sense. I felt the enormous relief.

The rain fell a little harder, applying gentle pressure on our conversation as we stood in the road.

"So Yar has a heart. I'm still not convinced but I'll go with it if you're saying he showed you tonight. Now let's get home before we start growing gills," Kevin said.

"Good idea, although I did want to ask you about Alice," I said with a smile.

Kevin stopped and took a couple of slow steps back in my direction.

"It's the strangest thing," he said, Kevin reaching for his next thought.

"Until recently all I wanted was to have Saira back but I don't think even the real Saira would live up to my memory of her."

Kevin paused.

"I hate myself for saying that, my biggest hope is she would understand and forgive me."

He took a deep breath then released it with a sigh.

"For the first time since she died I'm not looking back," Kevin said.

"I think she'd understand that Kev. I also think it's what she would want," I said in reply, gripping his upper arm firmly before my mind caught up with what my body had done.

10

"No one moves forward with their head in the sand."
Elon Mensch

9.38pm
Wednesday 23 April 2104
Session 10

THE FINAL GROUP session ended.

Kevin was there as always. Mila and Alice had stayed all the way through. Oran had dropped in for about 15 minutes. He looked well, talked continually then rushed out the door to catch up with friends who were celebrating Nepali New Year in Bhaktapur.

Mila was the next to leave now we were done. She hugged Alice and Kevin, held my hand for what seemed like ages and told all three of us how the last five months had been the best of her life.

Last week Alice had taken Mila on her first zip. She was still buzzing as she re-lived the experience.

"I can't believe I never did it before," Mila said, her eyes wide with excitement.

"I know everyone says it's impossible to feel yourself zipping, but I felt it happen."

Both of Mila's hands now covered mine as she spoke. It amazed me how this simple physical contact quieted the rest of my brain and held my attention. Mila had already described her trip in tonight's session but the storyteller in her was now reaching further, exploring the journey itself.

"I stepped into the pod, watched the lights go down until all I could see was pitch black. Then there was a light, a tiny pinprick way behind my eyes. At first I could hardly see it, then a hot white flash totally consumed me, and I scattered. I actually felt myself falling apart, atom-by-atom."

Mila mimed the scattering process, moving her fingers through the air as if she was playing a piano.

I'd heard other people talk about the journey part of ZJT but only in clichés. They were always flying, diving, blinded by light or staring into the eyes of god. In all my years of zip-travel I felt nothing. Not a single second of journey time or any other sensation. I knew Mila's story was impossible but like her fictional zip-stories it was enchanting, and she wasn't done yet.

"For the briefest moment I was everywhere. I was hanging in space. Infinite and serene is the only way to describe it. Then there was a jolt and I was nowhere. That was the strangest part, a distinct gap. Very different to the space that came before it."

For the briefest moment Mila looked puzzled, then her exuberance returned.

"And then I was being re-born. I felt the most incredible coming together. A wave of energy brought life back to my body. The impossible pattern of 'me' was re-emerging. Then I was whole again."

Mila paused for a second, her hands moved to cover her heart. We held each other's gaze as she thought.

"The most whole I've ever felt," she said.

I believed her. The intimacy between us surprised me. Mila had taken me on her journey. She wanted me to be part of it, perhaps she knew I was already part of it. I realised this was the closest I'd felt to anyone in years. For a split second I imagined us together. For the second time I pictured sharing my life with someone, instead of being alone.

Mila sensed something too. I guessed this when she looked away and because her cheeks flushed a little. One of Mila's hands stayed on her chest, playing with her necklace. I watched as the hammered, silver pendant rolled between her fingers.

"It's a good luck charm from Rajasthan," she said, aware I was looking.

"Alice and me are going back there tomorrow. Maybe you should come?"

It was a genuine invitation. Genuine but impossible for me to accept.

I thought about all the ways I wanted to reply.

"Maybe you and Alice can tell me about it when you get back?" was the best I could do.

I hoped Mila didn't take this as a no. There was no way for me to explain everything rushing through my mind. What I really wanted to say was, "To hell with it!" and go everywhere with Mila. Wherever she wanted. As many destinations as she could choose. I imagined us zipping around the world in a never-ending adventure.

"Maybe I could do it. Maybe it would be different this time?" I thought to myself.

Then the 'buts' and the dislocation kicked in, although I wasn't given time for the inward spiral to properly start.

"I'll hold you to that Steve," Mila answered my last question. "Message me your coordinates and I'll come and find you tomorrow."

Mila gave the three of us a broad smile before saying goodbye and heading for the door.

Throughout Mila's story Kevin had been smiling.

He came closer to me, clicking his fingers in front of my nose to make sure he had my full attention.

"Don't mess this up Steve, you've got a date."

Kevin laughed and clapped me hard between the shoulders.

"Careful Kevin, you'll knock his glasses off," Alice said, giggling at the pantomime playing out in front of her.

"But I don't wear glasses?" I said to Alice.

"I know Steve, but come on. You're the kind of guy who should," she said.

I had to admit that was funny.

In a double-act it's no bad thing to be the fall guy.

• • •

For what felt like it would be the last time, Kevin, Alice and I made the hall good.

The conversation had moved from Mila and me back to grounding and our recent sessions. Kevin was still on a high. It was the most animated I'd ever seen him on the subject of JT. He was also enjoying the extra time for reflection.

"You know Steve, I think you could make a career out of this if you wanted." Kevin said.

I laughed because he said the same thing as we walked home from my first JT session. Nothing could have been further from my mind at the time, but I also remember the idea didn't sound outrageous.

"Thanks for the vote of confidence Kev, it means even more this time around," I said in reply.

"I knew you'd remember. Do you forget anything we talk about?"

Kevin's reply was a joke but maybe a real question too. I smiled in response to both but he wasn't finished.

"Think about it for a moment. Another 5 people grounded, or at the very least five more people zipping with a new perspective on zip-travel. How many is that now? I don't care what anyone else thinks I know we make a difference."

Kevin was animated, really enjoying these positive thoughts.

"Maybe it makes a difference, maybe it doesn't," I said.

I was thinking aloud, my unguarded response surprised me. More was going on in my mind but none of it made sense. The return of zjt. The end of this programme. It all felt like a new beginning for everyone except me.

"Maybe Royar was right, this is the end of my little world," I thought to myself.

I shuddered as the image of a gloating look on Royar's face came to mind. Then I realised something. Despite my closeness to Mila's joy, Alice's happiness and to Kevin, my only real friend, I was alone.

I tried to shake the sick feeling rising from my stomach but the loneliness was overpowering. I thought about Kevin's point once again. Maybe he was still waiting for my answer. I asked myself again if what we did made any difference at all. Answering this question became an essential distraction.

Kevin had now moved away and was talking excitedly with Alice. I decided if he came back and pushed me for an answer, I would share what was on my mind.

I no longer had the strength to do anything else.

The answer I had at the ready was, "No. No I don't think we make any difference at all," but Kevin didn't come back and push.

• • •

As we left the hall I did my best to hide the way I was feeling.

After everything I've learned about sharing, I don't know why my default instinct is to hide. I was in a room with two people I felt comfortable with. Both of them had my trust completely. More than once I nearly said something but I couldn't find the words. All I wanted was Kevin and Alice's help but I couldn't find a way to say so out loud.

Perhaps it was my fear of the collapse that might follow.

The three of us moved into the porch. I turned off the lights, closed the inside door and started locking up.

"I've known you too long Steve," Kevin said out of the blue.

Maybe he was going to push me after all.

"I can tell by your face, your body language even. I know you think we don't make a difference but I'm telling you we do. Even if one person thinks differently about who and where they are, it makes grounding worthwhile." Kevin was sincere.

"He's right Steve. It does make a difference," Alice said, adding her weight to the conversation.

I wondered what Alice really thought of our little double act. Whether she liked, respected or pitied me. Whether she had sussed me as the hopeless case I am. I tried dismissing these harmful thoughts. In the end I remembered that unlike me, Alice wasn't afraid to embrace her emotions or speak her mind. If she felt any of this I would already know.

"These sessions have changed so much for me," Alice continued, "I couldn't tell you where I was before but I'm happy to be here right now, and that's a great start."

Alice looked like she meant what she was saying.

"It's good of you to say so Alice but what does it really mean? You're still the same person. How much can any of this really change you? All we did was talk. I'm not sure any of us even hear each other. We just hold on to what we think or what we want to hear."

I was confused. What I said was mixed up and definitely more than I wanted to say. This was also me whining, which frustrated me even more. I wanted Alice to understand and feel what I was feeling but I'd watered down my words. I no longer knew if I did this to protect her, or to protect me.

I half expected Alice to look hurt or at the very least a little taken aback by what I said but she wasn't affected in the slightest. I'd projected my own reaction once again.

"I'm not being nice to you Steve," Alice replied. "I didn't say any of this to make you feel better, this is how I feel. I feel more grounded. The programme made a difference to me."

"You're thinking too much again Steve," Kevin said, gently nudging me as we stood by the door.

"Listen to what Alice is saying. Ask yourself what Mila or Oran or even Royar would say. Maybe it doesn't change lives completely but we've definitely helped."

Kevin and Alice were trying to make me feel better but I wasn't ready to let my doubts go. The truth is I don't give myself a choice when it comes to letting go.

"Come on you two. We can walk and talk," Alice said, nestling further into Kevin's side.

Kevin looked a little apologetic and smiled, I slid the final bolt on the inside door.

"You go ahead, I'm not quite finished here," I said, although we all knew this was a lie.

Alice watched me a little closer. There was concern on her face but she was happy to follow Kevin's lead, for the moment at least. If there was a right time for me to tell Alice and Kevin how I was feeling, it was now.

A second or two of silence passed between us.

"Come on Steve, we've both seen you looking worse." Kevin said, tugging the shoulder of my jacket as he spoke.

He was trying to pull me towards them. Alice laughed as I nearly fell over.

I managed to keep my balance and the sullen look on my face despite a distant recess of my mind finding this funny too.

The moment for me to say something was lost.

• • •

In the end my protestations were enough, or Kevin and Alice just wanted to get going.

I resisted a final plea by pretending to struggle with the big padlock. Then I watched them both walk away. Alice's laughter faded as they walked. Their silhouettes bumped playfully together as they moved along the dimly lit path. If it was possible for silhouettes to look happy theirs did. I hoped this would always be the case. I hoped Alice and Kevin would be happy, together or apart.

I finished locking up the hall, turned away from the doors and glanced up. The night sky was glowing an unnatural smoky orange, up-lit by the city in the distance.

I started walking home. My mind wandered grimly, I gave in and let the thoughts flow.

"They're wrong. Grounding has no impact on our lives. The only reality is here and now. The path under my feet is real, the sound of my steps, the low beat of my heart. This is real."

In the silence I noticed how my steps seemed to keep time. They were regular, like the tick of an old fashioned clock.

I wondered why I felt so miserable. I tried to force myself to stop wallowing in grief. Unlike Kevin and Oran I hadn't experienced any real loss. I had no right to be feeling this way.

I don't know why but to break the spell I tried listening for my heartbeat, knowing it was there underneath.

I was desperate to connect with anything that felt real.

"Can I feel my heart? Really feel it, like Oran during his panic attack?" I thought to myself.

It took a while but I started to sense the rhythm that was there all along. I pressed my right hand over my chest and listened again as I walked. My breath became a new measure of time, slow and deep. The air flowed back and forth, up and down, in and out of my mouth and nose. I kept my mind focused on my body. I realised what an unusual thing this was for me to do. My attention didn't waver as I walked on. There was just me, my steps, my heart, my breath and the silences in between.

I listened again to the sounds my body was making. The brushing of my clothes added a muffled accompaniment of their own. Somehow it all fit together. The sound, the movement. But always with enough space for another new thought.

"What will my next thought be?"

I asked myself this question with a rising sense of anticipation. The lowness I was feeling began to melt away. With new energy my mind turned itself inwards. I imagined diving for new pearls of wisdom.

I tried to hold myself back.

"Don't force it. Not yet. Keep listening. Don't expect a revelation," I said to myself, but my heightened expectation remained.

Again, I thought about all the sounds I was making. I stared ahead, into the empty night. My forward-motion, time passing; it all framed a blank canvas. Colours and themes were mine to choose. It was the perfect space for me to fill.

"This is it," my thoughts found a voice once again.

"This is travel. This is walking. This is my time, my journey."

An overwhelming feeling washed over me. I thought about Mila's account of her zip. I thought again about the wholeness she mentioned. I saw the harmony in her eyes all over again. Maybe this was a time of answers for me too?

My thoughts continued, now gathering pace.

"This pace I am setting. This point in time. Finally I am where I want to be. Time, place, journey, destination. It all comes together now. I am here. I belong here, I want to be here, I..."

My cascading thoughts jolt to a standstill as a fox breaks cover from a hedge up ahead.

The sudden movement and glowing eyes stop me dead.

I watch in silence as the fox gazes in my direction, then emerges from the shadows and on to the footpath.

I can feel my euphoria ebbing away but instead of cursing the animal, I am transfixed.

Every step the fox takes is fascinating, fluid, balletic.

The fox lowers her head. She glances from side to side as she moves. Her paws track in perfect line.

She's gliding now.

Hugging the outline of a wall, her steps are impossibly light. The lithe form of the fox rises and falls in shallow, percussive beats. I realise the entire movement is perfect.

Somehow the fox's grace and purpose make me feel useless and insignificant again.

"I am truly powerless," my thoughts return with a lead-weighted blow.

The spirit of the fox put an end to my dreaming. What felt so real only seconds ago has disappeared back to nothing. The only thing that remains is my realisation of how false it all was.

I reach the kerb and step into the road, cursing myself as I do.

"Order is the greatest illusion. The only illusion I fall for again and again."

This is true, I think to myself.

"But there is no order. No human order reality can't break."

But still I can't forget how good the false order tastes. I can't stop myself striving for it or being fooled by its promise again and again in every part of my life.

Now my mind is beyond my control.

It jumps to doctors and medicine, I think how the scalpel is used to open up the human body and open the surgeon's eyes to impossible disorder yet perfect function at the same time. I think how all of science and human learning still leaves us short. How we will probably never completely understand the writhing mass of complexity inside us. To our greatest minds, despite our greatest efforts, beyond even our most miraculous technology, our bodies are living proof of a higher order. Something purely organic, perhaps always beyond our reach and permanently outside our control.

I realise the hall keys are still in my hand. I put them away and fish out my door card as I reach the garden path. I'm almost home but I keep thinking. Searching for some kind of closure at least, otherwise this will be another sleepless night.

"We all want life to go a certain way. Everyone wants life to make sense. We're so desperate for our lives to please us with essential things, like love and the closeness of friends. Like gods we want to be timeless and free. To cast no shadow and tread lightly on the ground. To feel the wind on our face and the sun on our skin. We want the sky, the clouds, the whole world to align perfectly, just for us. No change on the horizon. No passing of time. No end to our perfect state of grace."

I swallow hard past the lump in my throat.

"But none of that's real. All that's real is here and now. There are no other planes of existence. There is nothing in between. At some point all ideas are broken. In the meantime we fool ourselves to forget we are real."

With a tired sigh I arrive at my door.

"There is nothing beyond reality. No life outside of this moment. Nothing exists beyond this moment for me any more."

I am no less confused.

Standing still, I push the card into its reader.

The door opens, I step over the threshold and home.

Epilogue

IT DIDN'T TAKE long for the world to move on.

It still amazes me how quickly people trusted the new firmware. How swiftly the world went back to zip-travel. How soon all the losses were forgiven, maybe even forgotten by some.

When the grid came back online the pace of change was lightning fast. Quirky, small-batch pod hardware was rapidly phased out. The business of pod homogenisation became the latest ultra-growth market. New fortunes and great reputations have already been made as a result.

Elon Mensch has been a pioneer in this new market in a big way. Within the first few months of the grid coming back, he struck a deal to become the principal global hardware supplier for CdA and Virgin *Instant*. Elon also bought up second hand pods in their millions, re-selling the newly homologated stock, mainly to private grids in developing markets. In the developing and re-developing world the middle-class is growing rapidly. They're the ones with all the disposable income burning a hole in their pockets. They have the money, along with a ravenous appetite for a zjt-led lifestyle to go with it.

Elon's newest business also had a zero-waste strategy. Non-compliant hardware is recycled at a nice profit too. His roll-up effort has also stumbled upon the added bonus of a handful of pods with historic significance, although I would bet none of these discoveries were accidental. One or two of these finds have been kept for Elon's private collection. The rest have found their way into the permanent JT sponsored zip-time exhibit at Smithsonian Institutes on every continent.

One or two pods with really interesting technological solutions have been absorbed by JT's newly acquired R&D division, based at the old Apple headquarters in Cupertino, CA. The last thing I read was this is the lab Elon will be using to draw-up zjt standards for the next millennium.

You have to hand it to Elon, he knows how to sew up a market opportunity.

As for me, my next JT group kicks-off in two weeks, but there have been a few interesting changes in my local world too.

It was a tough choice but in the end Kevin decided to call it a day on his session work. It's possible he might come back to it in the future, but he seems happy enough to have left it behind for now. Kevin and I still see each other all the time. He still torments me without mercy, in between being back on the grid and busier than ever, picking up on all the projects that got left behind while zjt was down and the world stood still.

Kevin is also busy because he spends more of his time locally too. He's working on some big new projects in UK air, road and rail networks. Some people see it as a backward step but hard-travel re-captured the imagination during the shutdown. Kevin is finding that it's a good time to be a design and major projects engineer.

It's been great to see Kevin enjoying his time at home. I think Saira would be happy about this too. Kevin has been seeing a lot of Alice, especially now she is working from home. The last time I was round at his place, Alice told me her nephew was staying for the weekend. Unless Alice buys a dog in the next six months I think babysitting means there's only one thing Kevin can look forward to in the future.

I couldn't be happier for both of them if that's how things turn out, I've always fancied being an Uncle.

As for Kevin stepping away from JT, I can't think of anything else that could have made me more desperate, especially with a new programme just about to start. It won't be the same without him in the group. There I was, missing him already and we hadn't even started.

At first I had no idea how I was going to get through a whole grounding programme without Kevin keeping things calm. In my mind the group just wouldn't work without his experience on hand. The way he effortlessly breaks tension with smiles. His perfect comic timing and his ability to get away with saying the most inappropriate things. No one could replace Kevin in my mind.

When Kevin told me he was leaving I thought about doing the same. I always thought I would stay with Journey Time for years but that last group was different. I felt more grounded than ever when their programme came to an end, apart from my latest mini-bout of dislocation on my final walk home.

For a while I asked myself if I could ever connect with new group members the way I used to. Whether I could get personally involved all over again. Plus, doing it all without Kevin would be going beyond yet another comfort zone. Of course Kevin reckoned I'd be just fine without him. This helped a little but what really changed my mind was a call I received a few weeks ago from Royar of all people.

Kevin told Roy he was stepping down and that I was on the look-out for a new Vet.

"Believe me, I'm more surprised than you," Royar said when he called me.

"I could hardly stand to be there for most of my programme," he continued, confirming the obvious.

"Most of the time I had no idea why I was there but when it all finished and things went back to normal, something inside me had changed and there was no going back."

This was interesting but Royar's biggest revelation was still to come. He asked if we could meet for a drink. When we met up, Royar told me more about the aftermath of the last programme from his point of view.

"At first my mind kept drifting back to the group. Then, while I was travelling, I kept wondering what might be going on back in that crummy little hall. What were the new JT groups talking about? Had you and Kevin started your next group? What were the people like?"

It was beginning to sound like the set up to an elaborate practical joke. Kevin wasn't beyond crafting a wind-up as intricate as this. I decided there was no point trying to fight it, or guess where this was going. I just sat back, listened and let Royar speak, even if it meant being the fall guy again.

Royar continued.

"All of this was going through my mind when Kevin called to tell me he was stepping down. Kevin was stepping down and I was the first person he wanted to tell. I put two-and-two together and didn't even give him time to ask the question, I just said yes. The only missing piece of the puzzle is whether you'll have me as your Vet?"

I almost choked on my drink.

"Maybe you need a cynic like me to keep your feet on the ground?" Royar added with a Kevin-esque smile.

I could tell Royar wanted this, although it didn't take much guessing.

I wanted more time to think about my response but I already knew I was going to say yes.

"I don't know why but it just feels right," was how I summed up my feelings to Royar, dabbing my eyes and blowing beer foam out of my nose.

It wasn't dignified but inhaling my drink allowed me another few seconds think time. It was hard to explain but it was nonetheless true, the idea of Royar as my new Vet just felt right. All of the anxiety I had been feeling about the new group disappeared the moment Royar voiced the idea out loud.

I was even beginning to think this was an inspired piece of thinking by Kevin.

Despite everything that made Royar a terrible choice, I knew he was the right person for the role in my groups, and I knew he was motivated to learn. I didn't have to agree with Kevin and Royar but the more I thought about it, the more this solution made sense. Royar was the same person I had met at the start of the last programme but he was also different. He had proved this to himself. Kevin had seen a fundamental change in him and now so had I.

Without being able to express it, Royar felt all of this too. Maybe he knew the only way for the change in his life to continue was walking directly towards it. You can't run away from yourself, or as Elon also put it, "Burying your head in the sand just leaves you with grit in your eyes and your ass in the air."

For all his faults, and there were still plenty to pick from, Royar isn't the type to shy away.

It may have taken me too long to realise it, but neither am I.

Somehow this absurd idea also fit with the Journey Time philosophy. Who better to talk about the group programme and what it can achieve, than someone who entered the process as a cynic. Kevin had his doubts at the start. Royar had started with almost total disdain. That and a deep-seated, aggressive suspicion, not to mention an outright contempt for the entire JT organisation.

As Royar said when we finished talking, "What I have now isn't even a grudging respect for JT, I know grounding works. I want to take my grounding journey further, and I want to help others along the way."

Royar said this to me as the two of us stood in the middle of the road, talking exactly where Kevin and I always did.

I didn't get to speak my thoughts in response. My mind was wrestling with too many conflicting ideas, plus Royar still liked having the last word. Instead, I was happy thinking to myself how this was probably the clearest, closest view I'd ever get on personal choice in action. Royar was the archetypal hard-nosed follower of his own ideals but he willingly changed his mind, after giving himself a greater freedom to choose.

As Royar walked away I carried on thinking to myself but I couldn't come up with any better outcome than that.

And that would be the end of my story, but it is still only the third best thing to happen to me since I came to JT. The second best thing was meeting Kevin. The best thing without doubt has become Mila.

Mila and I have been seeing a lot of each other since the last programme ended. She now has had my permanent grid coordinates stored in her quad. Recently, Mila has picked up the new habit of zipping in to pods 30 seconds ahead of me. The first time she did it I nearly had a heart attack.

I told Mila my story about the fox. I told her all about it and the way it made me feel. How there was a moment in time when the fox was all I could think about or see. How this beautiful presence shattered the imaginary world I was living in.

I think that's why Mila zips to me. In fact I know that's why she does it. I think she likes to see the look on my face when she appears in front of me. Snapping me back to reality with the perfection of her walk and her eyes.

THE END

Glossary

AI IMPLANTS: (ARTIFICIAL Intelligence Implanting, AII) The science of mapping hypo-allergenic and/or Biomass™ memory modules and processors into human brains to deliver behavioural and subject-matter knowledge/experience. AII was pioneered by the team working under Dr. Mahendra S.R. Bose at the Indian Institute of Technology Delhi, in the late twenty-first century. The first successful human implant (an organically grown nano-flash chip) contained *The Complete Works of Shakespeare*, which the implanted subject (a Mr. Colin Chattarjee) was newly able to access and recite. Work on AI implanting now continues at a number of technology, science and medical institutes around the world, in pursuit of the breakthrough that will allow implanted subjects to travel via ZJT. [also called, Intra-Cranial Intellect Enhancement (ICIE)]

Amritsar: The Jallianwala Bagh massacre, also known as the Amritsar massacre, was a seminal event in the British rule of India. On 13 April 1919, a crowd of non-violent protesters, along with Baishakhi pilgrims, had gathered in the Jallianwala Bagh garden in Amritsar, Punjab, to protest the arrest of two leaders. On the orders of Brigadier-General Reginald Dyer, the army fired on the crowd. The dead numbered between 370 and 1,000, possibly more. The Amritsar massacre has often been cited as one of the main events leading to

India's movement towards independence from British rule in 1947. [Source: Wikipedia, 2014-2104, with amends]

anti-republique: A political and social movement, chiefly distinguished by the call to disband France and set up a series of independent, self-governing states. Some *'Contre-Républicanisme'* supporters took up an armed struggle after the French government outlawed the movement in 2068. The late-2103 attack at the new Paris Saint-Germain stadium is the movement's deadliest to-date. [also called, contre-republique, contre-républicanisme]

appeasement: Appeasement in a political context is a diplomatic policy of making political or material concessions to an enemy power in order to avoid conflict. The term is most often applied to the foreign policy of the British Prime Minister Neville Chamberlain towards Nazi Germany between 1937 and 1939. Appeasement's most famous twenty-first century application regards the international attitude towards Gazprom's progress towards an effective nuclear fusion monopoly between 2053 and 2071. [Source: Wikipedia, 2014-2104, with amends]

Apple: (Apple Inc.) US technology company founded in 1976, ceased trading in 2036 as the market for pre-quad personal device formats dried up. The one Apple-originated product still available today is the iPod 'Classic', manufactured and sold in limited, special-edition runs by the Samsung Consumer Electronics Group, Greater Korea.

big shutdown: The cessation of all ZJT-travel on July 31, 2101. [also called, 'the big switch-off'] [see also, IMA, Remod-c]

cancer: a historic wasting disease eradicated in the early part of the twenty-first century.

Chattarjee, Colin: The first human to be successfully implanted with an AI chip. At the time of his implant (April 14, 2071) Mr. Chattarjee was an IIT lab technician working alongside Dr. M.S.R. Bose. Following his implant, Mr. Chattarjee went on to have a successful career in the UK as one of The Royal Shakespeare Society's principal players. Mr. Chatterjee died in a freak narrow-boat accident in Stratford-upon-Avon, UK in 2099.

dreamtime: [also called, Alcheringa, The Dreamtime] In the mythology of some Australian Aborigines, the Dreamtime is the golden, spiritual age when the first ancestors and all life was created. [For more information on dreamtime, see *The Songlines* (1986) by Bruce Chatwin.

EST: (Eastern Standard Time) The time zone for New York City and the Eastern United States. Unless stated, all times in this story are GMT.

firmware: A set of permanent software instructions that form part of an electronic device and allow it to communicate with a computer or with other electronic devices via networks. In the case of ZJT, every pod variant requires its own unique firmware to join the grid and run the universal ZJTTP interface.

flow: Flow is the mental state of operation in which a person performing an activity is fully immersed in a feeling of energised focus, full involvement, and enjoyment in the process of the activity itself. In essence, flow is characterized by complete absorption in what one is doing. First proposed by Mihály Csíkszentmihályi in the twentieth-century, the positive psychology concept of 'flow' has since been widely expanded across a variety of fields. [Source: Wikipedia, 2014-2104, with amends]

forevermark: The global standard for recording and categorising gem diamonds, first used in the late twentieth-century, now owned and operated by The Diamond Caucus Ltd, an international trading and standards body headquartered in London and Moscow.

full-d: Informal colloquial term to describe peaks of dislocation in ZJT-d sufferers (e.g. 'I saw Camille last night. She hardly recognised me, I think she's full-d.'). [see ZJT-d for more]

fvc: (Firmware Version Conflict) Traced as the cause of IMA, finally accepted as the universal cause in December 2100, leading to the cessation of all ZJT-travel in July 2101. Pre-homologated pod hardware required its own unique firmware to run ZJTTP, join the grid and 'handshake' with pods from different manufacturers. While ZJTTP took care of the modulation and re-modulation of physical matter at each end of a zip-travel journey, minor variations and conflicts in pod firmwares caused imperfections in living organisms (at cellular levels), later categorised and diagnosed as Remod-c (RC) and IMA.

Gaga IV, Lady: (Ms. Drayon Gaga-Germanotta, aka Lady Gaga IV). World famous performer, music and arts magnate; Owner of Gaga-Global; Great-Granddaughter of the original Lady Gaga; ***1 on the Farbes' Global Billionaires Rich-List every year since 2073*. [*Source: Farbes & Faber Global Wealth Management Corp, 2073-2104]

GMT: (Greenwich Mean Time) The standard time zone for the UK.

grid: Common name for the ZJT network. The word 'grid' can be used for any public or private zip-travel service, service provider or network. The largest public service providers globally include, Greyhound, CdA (China Digital Air), Z00P:0) and Virgin *Instant*. Notable private grids include, Fleetway, Step'N'Go and TaG.

handbook: 'The Official Journey Time Handbook' was written by Elon Mensch and published soon after his acquisition of Journey Time Inc. in December 2099. The handbook contains all of JT's corporate values, regulations, procedures, cultural and behavioural ideals, plus an outline of the entire 5 month grounding group programme. In a New York Times interview in 2102, Mensch claimed he wrote all 90,000 words of the JT handbook in one long-weekend. In the same interview he cited his inspiration as, "the personal impact of the grounding process" as well as, "the need to standardise the programme and ensure every participant's experience is the same". In January 2104, Mensch said his model for the JT handbook was an old copy of KFC's daily operations manual he found among family articles in storage.

hard-travel: Informal collective term for all pre-ZJT modes of travel (e.g. walking, bike, car, rail, sea, air). Hard-travel made a rapid comeback during the shutdown years (2101-2104), and although usage continues to be higher than pre-shutdown levels, hard-travel is still seen by most as unnecessary journey time.

IMA: (Irreversible Modem Aptosis) The medical name for RC. IMA, or irreversible cellular death, is now known to be caused by version conflicts in ZJT pod firmware [see FVC]. Worldwide IMA deaths are currently estimated at three million, with six million terminally infected (Source: WHO 2102). New incidences of IMA were effectively eradicated by the July 2101 cessation of all ZJT-travel. Second stage and final eradication followed the 2103 release of a new universal ZJT firmware and global hardware homologation programme. [see also, Remod-c]

intrusive thoughts: Unwelcome involuntary thoughts, images, or unpleasant ideas that may become obsessions, are upsetting or distressing, and can be difficult to manage or eliminate. When they are associated with obsessive-compulsive disorder (OCD), depression, body dysmorphic disorder (BDD), and sometimes attention-deficit hyperactivity disorder (ADHD), the thoughts may become paralyzing, anxiety-provoking, or persistent. Intrusive thoughts may also be associated with episodic memory, unwanted worries or memories from OCD, posttraumatic stress disorder (PTSD), other anxiety disorders, eating disorders, psychosis and ZJT-d (Zero Journey Time Dislocation Syndrome). [Source: Wikipedia, 2014-2104, with amends]

Journey Time: (NYSE: JYT) The international organisation initially set up as a support network for sufferers of ZJT-d. Journey Time International Inc. is now the largest privately owned business in the world (excluding Asia), rising to prominence following the July 2101 cessation of all ZJT-travel. Journey Time's CEO and majority owner Elon Mensch acquired the company in late-2099 in an outright purchase described as 'friendly' by most market commentators at the time. [also called, JT, Journey Time™, JT™]

KFC: A historic business primarily made up of fast-food counters selling fried chicken, famous in the late twentieth and early twenty-first centuries. Although highly successful the company entered Chapter 11 bankruptcy in August 2022 after a combination of factors contributed to rapid decline and ultimate foreclosure. Chief among the factors behind KFC's demise were: (i) Obesity's classification as a global epidemic (October 2015), (ii) Worldwide shortages in chicken, following repeated outbreaks of HPAI (Highly-Pathogenic Avian Influenza or 'Bird Flu') (2012-2035). (iii) KFC's disastrous move into theme parks (e.g. KFC'hickenLand, Cincinnati, Ohio), leisure cruises (KFSeas 'Cruise with The Colonel' LLC) and custom automobiles (Harland Sanders' Breast Roast Customs Inc.). [also known as, Kentucky Fried Chicken]

Mensch Calculation, The: ($v = \$ \div t$) Value equals Money divided by Time. According to Elon Mensch, this calculation can and should be applied to any task, decision or endeavor, in order to keep one's aspirations for financial accumulation in check.

Mensch, Elon: Entrepreneur, businessman, philanthropist, best-selling author, social activist and self-proclaimed 'Global Learning Advocate', Elon S. E. (Stephenson Edison) Mensch is perhaps best known as the CEO and majority shareholder of Journey Time International Inc. Mr Mensch's other major business interests include ownership and life-chair of MTR International, the world's third largest ZJT-pod manufacturing business (as measured by active pod status in 2100).

quad-gpd: (Quartered Access Device - Grid Point Device) Generic, non-manufacturer specific term for the most commonly used communication, location and multi-purpose personal device. The standard format for a quad is a 10" tablet that can be folded in half and used as a 'phone', and folded in half-again for portability. Notable quad manufacturers include Handi GmbH, Samsung and WalianGCI. [also called, QuAD, QAD, quad, gpd].

RC: (Remodulation Cancer) The common name in use for IMA, despite the mistaken connection between IMA and Cancer, which pre-dated the final medical classification of the disease. The name

RC was coined because the symptoms of IMA were initially believed to be a type of cancer. [also called, Remod-c, Transfer Cancer].

Vet: The Veteran system was an original component of the Journey Time grounding programme, although it was elevated to its permanent and central place in every group by Elon Mensch. Lady Gaga IV has made a well-known, often repeated claim to being the JT Vet in Elon Mensch's first grounding group. Although Gaga IV has repeated this claim often, and told anecdotal stories about some of the exchanges she claims to have heard, her claim has never been substantiated. Official comment from Journey Time Inc, Elon Mensch and his representatives has been absolute and consistent denial.

walk: During zip-travel's first phase, there was a growing general fear that the art of walking would be lost. Among the more extreme predictions at this time, was the suggestion that the human race would lose the ability to walk altogether. The shutdown years changed the tone of public and academic dialogues on walking. With no access to zjt, populations became more sedentary, greater localisation of work, consumption and leisure-time took place, as did a resurgence of walking. With the resumption of zip-travel in March 2104, a new popular, philosophical and artistic interest in walking was born. New social, commercial and cultural activities (around walking) began to spring up. Some leading academics have called this movement a return to the origins of human-centric journey-time. People less inclined to intellectualise this phenomenon have called it 'Global Pedestrianism' and 'The New Pedestrian Age'. Colloquially, the return to walking is referred to as, 'going outdoors and getting off your ass'. [also called, perambulating, promenading, strolling, riding on Shank's pony]

Where are YOU?: Archives suggest Royar was referring to a 1968 edition of *Analog* magazine, with artwork by Frank Kelly Freas. If Royar's recollections are correct, his Granddad's magazine would be the only known copy still in existence. With the value of mid-twentieth century science fiction recently reaching its highest ever point, experts have valued this original edition at over €45m.

Yar's Revenge: Yar's Revenge was originally a video game released for the Atari 2600 home entertainment console in 1982. Although the historical significance of the game itself was largely contemporary, the name 'Yar' has cropped up in more recent subcultures, each time with different meanings. For example, in late twenty-first century Kenyan slang, 'Yar' is a derogatory term for a certain type of tourist (typically: wealthy, sunburnt, loud, unfit and displaying little common sense). In the North of England 'Yar' is also a name given to 'flashy Southern folk' for their propensity to talk loudly into their quads, nodding their heads and saying 'Yar, yar' in loud voices. [Source: Weiner & Schnitzel's Colloquial Compendium, 2104]

ZJT: (Zero Journey Time) The common name in use for digital point-to-point travel for people and materials via data networks. [also called, zjt-travel, zip-travel, zip, zipping, zee-time]

ZJTTP: (The Helsinki Open-Source Zero Journey Time Transport Protocol) The standardised data transport protocol used by the global grid in the modulation and re-modulation of all physical matter transported via ZJT. [also called, zjttp://]

ZJT-d: (Zero Journey Time Dislocation Syndrome) The first medical syndrome diagnosed with ZJT as its cause. Sufferers of ZJT-d find it hard to establish and maintain a connection with physical locations and/or people. Symptoms also include anxiety, panic attacks and in extreme cases personality-disorders. Symptoms of ZJT-d are exclusively psychological. They are also directly related to factors including, continual zip-travel over extended periods, excessive zip-travel or, conversely, a lack of access to the grid. Although ZJT-d is a global phenomenon, the numbers of people affected and the ability of most sufferers to function normally, means the medical classification of dislocation syndromes is neither serious nor life threatening. ZJT-d is perhaps most famous for being the original catalyst for the founding of Journey Time and for never having a single instance in Greater Ireland. [see also, Full-d]

Paul Diamond: A lifelong fan of science-fiction and the genre's ability to liberate thoughts on society and the human condition, Journey Time is Paul's first novel. The literary influences he cites for this work include Albert Camus, Voltaire, George Orwell, Jonathan Swift, Philip K. Dick and John Steinbeck. Originally from East London, Paul now lives in Hertfordshire with his wife, daughter and two (generally) well-behaved dogs.

Printed in Great Britain
by Amazon.co.uk, Ltd.,
Marston Gate.